is to be returned on or before
ast date stamped below.

CHRISTMAS:
A CELEBRATION

CHRISTMAS
A CELEBRATION

John Rhodes

faber and faber
LONDON · BOSTON

First published in 1986
by Faber and Faber Limited
3 Queen Square, London WC1N 3AU

Photoset by Goodfellow & Egan Ltd, Cambridge.

Printed in Great Britain by
Mackays of Chatham Ltd, Kent

British Library Cataloguing in Publication Data

Christmas: a celebration.
1. Childrens literature, English
2. Christmas. —— Literary collections
I. Rhodes, John
820.8'033   PR1111.C53
ISBN 0-571-13752-0

Library of Congress Cataloguing-in-Publication Data

Christmas, a celebration.

Summary: An anthology of works by a variety of authors
describing ways in which Christmas has been celebrated
throughout the ages.
1. Christmas—Juvenile literature. [1. Christmas]
I. Rhodes, John, 1940–
GT4985.5.C48   1986   394.2'68282   86-9006
ISBN 0-571-13752-0

Contents

Foreword

In choosing material for this anthology, I have been guided by two main principles.

First, I wanted to present a series of extracts which would give an overall view of the way in which Christmas has been celebrated over the past few centuries; after a brief introductory section which groups together a number of reflective pieces on the meaning of Christmas, the material of the second, longer, section is therefore arranged in chronological form, from mediaeval to modern times.

Secondly, I have tried to select pieces which reflect the differing styles of writing of each period, and although, as a result, some of the extracts may now read rather quaintly or archaically, I feel they justify their inclusion by giving an accurate feeling of contemporary thought and expression.

Brief biographical and background notes are given by way of introduction to each extract.

J.R.

Acknowledgements

'Christmas Day' by Andrew Young from *The Poetical Works of Andrew Young*, reprinted by permission of Secker & Warburg Ltd.

A scene from *The Man Born to be King* by Dorothy L. Sayers, reprinted by permission of Gollancz Ltd.

'Ballad of the Bread Man' by Charles Causley from *Collected Poems*, reprinted by permission of Macmillan Ltd.

'The Eve of Christmas' by James Kirkup, reprinted by permission of the author.

An extract reprinted from *The Lore and Language of Schoolchildren* by Iona and Peter Opie (1959) by permission of Oxford University Press.

An extract from *The Sword in the Stone* by T.H. White, published by William Collins Sons & Co Ltd.

An extract from *Kilvert's Diary* edited by William Plomer, published by Jonathan Cape Ltd, reprinted by permission of Mrs Sheila Hooper.

An extract reprinted from *Lark Rise to Candleford* by Flora Thompson (1954) by permission of Oxford University Press.

'Christmas in India' by Rudyard Kipling from *The Definitive Edition of Rudyard Kipling's Verse*, reprinted by permission of The National Trust and Macmillan London, Ltd.

An extract from *Cider with Rose* by Laurie Lee, reprinted by permission of The Hogarth Press.

An extract from *William's Truthful Christmas* from *Still William* by Richmal Crompton, reprinted by permission of Mrs Richmal Ashbee.

Christmas with the Cheggies from *Mother Knew Best* by Dolly Scannell, reprinted by permission of the author.

An extract from *The Diary of a Provincial Lady* by E.M. Delafield, reprinted by permission of A.D. Peters & Co Ltd.

An extract from *Yorkshire Relish* by Elizabeth Cragoe, reprinted by permission of Hamish Hamilton Ltd.

An extract from *About my Father's Business* by Lilian Beckwith, reprinted by permission of the Hutchinson Publishing Group Ltd.

An extract reprinted by permission of Macmillan Publishing Company from *Whatever Happened to Tom Mix?* originally published by Cassell & Co Ltd. © Ted Willis 1970.

An extract from *A Child's Christmas in Wales* by Dylan Thomas, published by J.M. Dent & Sons Ltd.

Albert and the Liner from *Mondays, Thursdays* by Keith Waterhouse, published by Michael Joseph Ltd.

African Christmas by John Press, reprinted by permission of the author.

An extract from *The G.I.s* by Norman Longmate, reprinted by permission of the author.

An extract from *Village Diary* by 'Miss Read', reprinted by permission of Michael Joseph Ltd.

'I've had a Lousy Xmas' by Roger McGough from *The Liverpool Scene*, edited by Edward Lucie-Smith (1967), reprinted by permission of André Deutsch Ltd.

An extract from *The Solitary Landscape* by Edward Storey, published by Victor Gollancz Ltd.

'Christmas' by John Betjeman from *Collected Poems* reprinted by permission of John Murray (Publishers) Ltd.

1

King Herod and the Cock

This anonymous mediaeval poem shows all the strength of traditional English ballads, in its robust and direct language and its simple but vivid central incident, admirably portraying the miracle of Christmas.

There was a star in David's land,
In David's land did appear:
And in King Herod's chamber
So bright it did shine there.

The Wise Men they soon spied it,
And told the King a-nigh
That a princely babe was born that night,
No King shall e'er destroy.

'If this be the truth,' King Herod said,
'That thou hast told to me,
The roasted cock that lies in the dish
Shall crow full senses[1] three.'

O the cock soon thrustened[2] and feathered well,
By the work of God's own hand,
And he did crow full senses three,
In the dish where he did stand.

---

[1]Senses = times
[2]Thrustened = thrived; came to life

A Carol

ROBERT HERRICK

Robert Herrick (1591–1674) spent the first ten years of his working life as apprentice to his uncle, a goldsmith, but after graduating from Cambridge he entered the ministry and eventually became rector of Dean Prior in Devon in 1629. Herrick's 'Carol', like the previous piece, celebrates in deceptively simple style the central Christian tenet of the supreme significance of the birth of Christ.

What sweeter music can we bring
Than a carol for to sing
The birth of this our heav'nly King.
Awake the voice! Awake the string!
Dark and dull night fly hence away,
And give the honour of this day,
That sees December turned to May.

If we may ask the reason, say
The why and wherefore all things here
Seem like the Springtime of the year?
Why does the chilling Winter's morn,
Smile like a field beset with corn?
We see him come and know Him ours,
Who with His sunshine and His showers
Turns all the patient ground to flowers.

The Darling of the world is come,
And fit it is we find a room
To welcome Him. The nobler part
Of all the house here is the heart,
Which we will give Him and bequeath
This holly and this ivy wreath,
To do Him honour who's our King
And Lord of all this revelling.

3

from
Ben-Hur

LEW WALLACE

*When Major-General Lew Wallace's story **Ben-Hur: A Tale of the Christ** first appeared, it was an instant success. The potential of the story for the cinema screen was soon noted, and the silent-film version of the book (costing four million dollars and notable for its exciting chariot-race sequence) was released in 1926. The remake in 1959 proved that the story had lost none of its power, and the film was the smash hit of the year, winning no fewer than eleven Oscars.*
The extract is from the early chapters of the book, dealing with the birth of Christ.

A mile and a half, it may be two miles, south-east of Bethlehem, there is a plain separated from the town by an intervening swell of the mountain. At the side farthest from the town, close under a bluff, there was an extensive *mârâh*, or sheepcot, ages old. In some long-forgotten foray, the building had been unroofed and almost demolished. The enclosure attached to it remained intact, however, and that was of more importance to the shepherds who drove their charges thither than the house itself.

The day of the occurrences which occupy the preceding chapters, a number of shepherds, seeking fresh walks for their flocks, led them up to this plain; and from early morning the groves had been made ring with calls, and the blows of axes, the bleating of sheep and goats, the tinkling of bells, the lowing of cattle, and the barking of dogs. When the sun went down, they led the way to the *mârâh*, and by nightfall had everything safe in the field; then they kindled a fire down by the gate, partook of their humble supper, and sat down to rest and talk, leaving one on watch.

There were six of these men, omitting the watchman; and after-while they assembled in a group near the fire, some sitting, some lying prone.

Such were the shepherds of Judea! In appearance, rough and savage as the gaunt dogs sitting with them around the blaze; in fact, simple-minded, tender-hearted; effects due, in part, to the primitive life they led, but chiefly to their constant care of things lovable and helpless.

While they talked, and before the first watch was over, one by one the shepherds went to sleep, each lying where he had sat.

By the gate, hugging his mantle close, the watchman walked; at times he stopped attracted by a stir among the sleeping herds, or by a jackal's cry off on the mountain-side. The midnight was slow coming to him; but at last it came. His task was done; now for the dreamless sleep with which labour blesses its wearied children! He moved towards the fire, but paused; a light was breaking around him, soft and white, like the moon's. He waited breathlessly. The light deepened; things before invisible came to view; he saw the whole field, and all it sheltered. A chill sharper than that of the frosty air – a chill of fear – smote him. He looked up; the stars were gone; the light was dropping as from a window in the sky; as he looked, it became a splendour; then, in terror, he cried,–

'Awake, awake!'

Up sprang the dogs, and, howling, ran away.

The herds rushed together bewildered.

The men clambered to their feet, weapons in hand.

'What is it?' they asked in one voice.

'See!' cried the watchman, 'the sky is on fire!'

Suddenly the light became intolerably bright, and they covered their eyes, and dropped upon their knees; then, as their souls shrank with fear, they fell upon their faces blind and fainting, and would have died had not a voice said to them,

'Fear not!'

And they listened.

'Fear not: for, behold, I bring you good tidings of great joy, which shall be to all people.'

The voice, in sweetness and soothing more than human, and low and clear, penetrated all their being, and filled them with assurance. They rose upon their knees, and, looking worshipfully, beheld in the centre of a great glory the appearance of a man, clad in a robe intensely white; above its shoulders towered the tops of wings shining and folded; a star over its forehead glowed with steady lustre, brilliant as Hesperus; its hands were stretched towards them in blessing; its face was serene and divinely beautiful.

They had often heard, and, in their simple way, talked, of angels; and they doubted not now, but said in their hearts, The glory of

God is about us, and this is he who of old came to the prophet by the river of Ulai.

Directly the angel continued,–

'For unto you is born this day, in the city of David, a Saviour, which is Christ the Lord!'

Again there was a rest, while the words sank into their minds.

'And this shall be a sign unto you,' the annunciator said next. 'Ye shall find a babe, wrapped in swaddling-clothes, lying in a manger.'

The herald spoke not again; his good tidings were told; yet he stayed awhile. Suddenly the light, of which he seemed the centre, turned roseate and began to tremble; then up, far as the men could see, there was flashing of white wings, and coming and going of radiant forms, and voices as of a multitude chanting in unison,–

'Glory to God in the highest, and on earth peace, goodwill towards men!'

Not once the praise, but many times.

Then the herald raised his eyes as seeking approval of one far off; his wings stirred, and spread slowly and majestically, on their upper side white as snow, in the shadow vari-tinted, like mother-of-pearl; when they were expanded many cubits beyond his stature, he arose lightly, and, without effort, floated out of view, taking the light up with him. Long after he was gone, down from the sky fell the refrain in measure mellowed by distance, 'Glory to God in the highest, and on earth peace, goodwill towards men.'

When the shepherds came fully to their senses, they stared at each other stupidly, until one of them said, 'It was Gabriel, the Lord's messenger unto men.'

None answered.

'Christ the Lord is born; said he not so?'

Then another recovered his voice, and replied, 'That is what he said.'

'And did he not also say, in the city of David, which is our Bethlehem yonder. And that we should find Him a babe in swaddling-clothes?'

'And lying in a manger.'

The first speaker gazed into the fire thoughtfully, but at length said, like one possessed of a sudden resolve, 'There is but one place in Bethlehem where there are mangers; but one, and that is in the cave near the old khan. Brethren, let us go see this thing which has come to pass. The priests and doctors have been a long time looking for the Christ. Now He is born, and the Lord has given us a sign by which to know Him. Let us go up and worship Him.'

'But the flocks!'

'The Lord will take care of them. Let us make haste.'

Then they all arose and left the *mârâh*.

Around the mountain and through the town they passed, and came to the gate of the khan, where there was a man on watch.

'What would you have?' he asked.

'We have seen and heard great things to-night,' they replied.

'Well, we, too, have seen great things, but heard nothing. What did you hear?'

'Let us go down to the cave in the enclosure, that we may be sure; then we will tell you all. Come with us, and see for yourself.'

'It is a fool's errand.'

'No, the Christ is born.'

'The Christ! How do you know?'

'Let us go and see first.'

The man laughed scornfully.

'The Christ indeed. How are you to know Him?'

'He was born this night, and is now lying in a manger, so we were told; and there is but one place in Bethlehem with mangers.'

'The cave?'

'Yes. Come with us.'

They went through the court-yard without notice, although there were some up even then talking about the wonderful light. The door of the cavern was open. A lantern was burning within, and they entered unceremoniously.

'I give you peace,' the watchman said to Joseph and the Beth-Dagonite. 'Here are people looking for a Child born this night, whom they are to know by finding Him in swaddling-clothes and lying in a manger.'

For a moment the face of the stolid Nazarene was moved; turning away, he said, 'The Child is here.'

They were led to one of the mangers, and there the Child was. The lantern was brought, and the shepherds stood by mute. The little one made no sign; it was as others just born.

'Where is the mother?' asked the watchman.

One of the women took the baby, and went to Mary, lying near, and put it in her arms. Then the bystanders collected about the two.

'It is the Christ!' said a shepherd at last.

'The Christ!' they all repeated, falling upon their knees in worship. One of them repeated several times over,–

'It is the Lord, and His glory is above the earth and heaven.'

And the simple men, never doubting, kissed the hem of the mother's robe, and with joyful faces departed. In the khan, to all the people aroused and pressing about them, they told their story; and through the town, and all the way back to the *mârâh*, they chanted the refrain of the angels, 'Glory to God in the highest, and on earth peace, goodwill towards men!'

The story went abroad, confirmed by the light so generally seen; and the next day, and for days thereafter, the cave was visited by curious crowds, of whom some believed, though the greater part laughed and mocked.

4

from
The Wakefield
Second Shepherds' Pageant

*The early fifteenth-century **Second Shepherds' Pageant**, part of the Wakefield cycle of plays, is the work of an unknown author. The first part of the pageant is knockabout farce, and concerns the stealing of a sheep by Mak, who then hides it in a cradle and tries to pass it off as his new-born son; the theme thus parallels the Nativity theme of the second part of the play, printed below. The Shepherds are discussing the sheep-stealing episode and the two thieves, Mak and his wife, at the opening of this extract.*

The original language has been retained, since any attempt to translate into modern English is detrimental to the unique rhyme scheme and stanza structure, but some of the more obscure words and phrases are glossed.

SCENE 7. *The open fields*

1 SHEP.   Lord, what I am sore, in point for to burst!
    In faith, I may no more; therefore will I rest.

2 SHEP.   As a sheep of seven score he weighed in my fist.
    For to sleep aywhere methink that I list.[1]

3 SHEP.   Now I pray you
    Lie down on this green.

1 SHEP.   On these thieves yet I mean.[2]

3 SHEP.   Whereto should ye teen?[3]
    Do as I say you.

---

[1] list: would like
[2] mean: think
[3] teen: bother yourself

An Angel sings 'Gloria in excelsis,' and then says:

ANGEL.   Rise, herdmen hend,[4] for now is he born
   That shall take from the fiend that Adam had
      lorn;[5]
   That warlock to shend,[6] this night is he born.
   God is made your friend now at this morn,
   He behests.[7]
   At Bedlem[8] go see
   There lies that free[9]
   In a crib full poorly,
   Betwixt two beasts.
1 SHEP.   This was a quaint steven[10] that
      ever yet I heard.
   It is a marvel to neven,[11] thus to be scared.
2 SHEP.   Of God's son of heaven he spoke upward.
   All the wood on a leven methought that he gard
      Appear.[12]
3 SHEP.   He spake of a bairn
   In Bedlem, I you warn.
1 SHEP.   That betokens yond starn;
   Let us seek him there.
2 SHEP.   Say, what was his song? Heard ye not how
      he cracked it,
   Three breves to a long?
3 SHEP.   Yea, marry, he hacked it:
   Was no crochet long, nor no thing that lacked it.
1 SHEP.   For to sing us among, right as he
      knacked[13] it,
   I can.

---

[4]hend: gentle
[5]that Adam had lorn: what Adam lost
[6]that warlock to shend: in order to destroy that devil
[7]behests: promises
[8]Bedlem: Bethlehem
[9]free: gracious one
[10]steven: voice
[11]neven: relate
[12]All the wood . . . Appear: I thought he made the whole wood light up
[13]knacked: sang

2 SHEP.   Let see how ye croon.
       Can ye bark at the moon?
3 SHEP.   Hold your tongues! Have done!
1 SHEP.   Hark after, then.   [*Sings.*
2 SHEP.   To Bedlem he bade that we should gang;
       I am full adrad that we tarry too long.
3 SHEP.   Be merry and not sad – of mirth is our song!
       Everlasting glad to meed may we fang[14]
       Without noise.
1 SHEP.   Hie we thither forthy,
       If we be wet and weary,
       To that child and that lady,
       We have it not to lose.
2 SHEP.   We find by the prophecy – let be your
          din![15]–
       Of David and Isay, and more than I
          min[16]–
       They prophesied by clergy – that in a virgin
       Should he light and lie, to sloken[17] our sin,
       And slake it,
       Our kind, from woe;
       For Isay said so:
       Ecce virgo
       Concipiet a child that is naked.
3 SHEP.   Full glad may we be, and abide that day
       That lovely to see, that all mights may.[18]
       Lord, well were me for once and for ay,
       Might I kneel on my knee, some word for to say
       To that child.
       But the angel said
       In a crib was he laid;
       He was poorly arrayed,
       Both meek and mild.

---

[14]Everlasting glad . . . fang: We can get everlasting happiness as a reward
[15]let be your din!: stop your noise!
[16]min: remember
[17]sloken: atone for
[18]that all mights may: that can do anything

1 SHEP. Patriarchs that have been, and prophets beforn,
They desired to have seen this child that is born.
They are gone full clean;[19] that have they lorn.
We shall see him, I ween, ere it be morn,
To token.[20]
When I see him and feel,
Then wot I full well
It is true as steel
That prophets have spoken:

To so poor as we are that he would appear,
First find, and declare by his messenger.
2 SHEP. Go we now, let us fare; the place is us near.
3 SHEP. I am ready and yare;[21] go we infere[22]
To that bright.
Lord, if thy will be–
We are lewd[23] all three–
Thou grant us some kins glee
To comfort thy wight.[24]

Scene 8. *The stable in Bethlehem*

1 SHEP. Hail, comely and clean; hail, young child!
Hail, made,[25] as I mean, of a maiden so mild!
Thou hast waried,[26] I ween, the warlock so wild:
The false guiler of teen,[27] now goes he beguiled.
Lo, he merries,
Lo, he laughs, my sweeting!
A well fare meeting!
I have holden my heting:[28]
Have a bob[29] of cherries.

---

[19]full clean: completely
[20]to token: as a sign
[21]yare: eager
[22]infere: together
[23]lewd: simple
[24]Thou grant . . . thy wight: Grant us some happy way to comfort your child
[25]made of: born of
[26]waried: tricked
[27]The false guiler of teen: the false deceiver (ie. the Devil)
[28]holden my heting: kept my word
[29]bob: bunch

2 SHEP.   Hail, sovereign saviour, for thou hast us
      sought!
    Hail, freely food and flower, that all thing hast
      wrought!
    Hail, full of favour, that made all of nought!
    Hail! I kneel and I cower. A bird have I brought
    To my bairn.
    Hail, little tiny mop!
    Of our creed thou art crop;[30]
    I would drink on thy cop,[31]
    Little day-starn.

3 SHEP.   Hail, darling dear, full of Godhead!
    I pray thee be near when that I have need.
    Hail, sweet is thy cheer! My heart would bleed
    To see thee sit here in so poor weed,[32]
    With no pennies.
    Hail! Put forth thy dall![33]
    I bring thee but a ball:
    Have and play thee withal,
    And go to the tennis.

MARY.   The Father of heaven, God omnipotent,
    That set all on seven,[34] his Son has he sent.
    My name could he neven,[35] and light ere he
      went.[36]
    I conceived him full even through might, as he
      meant;
    And now is he born.
    He keep you from woe!–
    I shall pray him so.
    Tell forth as ye go,
    And min on this morn.

---

[30]Of our creed thou art crop: You are the head of our faith
[31]on thy cop: from your cup
[32]weed: clothes
[33]dall: hand
[34]That set all on seven: Who created everything in seven days
[35]neven: name
[36]light ere he went: shone brightly before he departed

1 SHEP.   Farewell, lady, so fair to behold,
    With thy child on thy knee.
2 SHEP.   But he lies full cold.
    Lord, well is me! Now we go, thou behold.
3 SHEP.   Forsooth, already it seems to be told
    Full oft.
1 SHEP.   What grace we have fun![37]
2 SHEP.   Come forth; now are we won![38]
3 SHEP.   To sing are we bun:[39]
    Let take on loft.[40]

---

[37] fun: found
[38] won: redeemed
[39] bun: obliged
[40] Let take on loft: let us sing loudly

5

Christmas Day

ANDREW YOUNG

Andrew Young (1885–1971) developed an interest in the countryside and in wild flowers in particular while he was still a boy: this latter study grew into a life-long hobby, and he wrote two authoritative books on the subject. Recognition as a poet came relatively late: he was awarded the Queen's Gold Medal for poetry in 1952 and his **Collected Poems** *appeared in 1960. His style is deceptively simple, and his subject-matter is in the tradition of those other close observers of the countryside, Clare, Hardy and Edward Thomas.*

Last night in the open shippen
    The Infant Jesus lay,
While cows stood at the hay-crib
    Twitching the sweet hay.

As I trudged through the snow-fields
    That lay in their own light,
A thorn-bush with its shadow
    Stood doubled on the night.

And I stayed on my journey
    To listen to the cheep
Of a small bird in the thorn-bush
    I woke from its puffed sleep.

The bright stars were my angels
    And with the heavenly host
I sang praise to the Father,
    The Son and Holy Ghost.

6

The Oxen

THOMAS HARDY

According to Robert Graves, Thomas Hardy valued his poetry more highly than his novel-writing, having to work hard at the latter whereas poems came to him, he said, 'by accident'. This poem, written in 1915, has its origins in an old country belief that on Christmas Eve the animals gather in attitudes of worship as a re-enactment of the original events in the stable at Bethlehem.

Christmas Eve, and twelve of the clock.
'Now they are all on their knees,'
An elder said as we sat in a flock
By the embers in hearthside ease.

We pictured the meek mild creatures where
They dwelt in their strawy pen,
Nor did it occur to one of us there
To doubt they were kneeling then.

So fair a fancy few would weave
In these years! Yet, I feel,
If someone said on Christmas Eve,
'Come; see the oxen kneel

In the lonely barton by yonder coomb
Our childhood used to know,'
I should go with him in the gloom,
Hoping it might be so.

from
The Man Born to be King

DOROTHY L. SAYERS

In 1940 Dorothy L. Sayers, creator of the aristocratic detective Lord Peter Wimsey, was invited by the BBC to write a series of plays on the life of Christ for broadcasting in the Sunday 'Children's Hour'. In the end, twelve plays were written, and put on the air between December 1941 and October 1942. One of the conditions which Miss Sayers laid down was that the plays should be realistic and use modern speech, an approach that led to some controversy at the time. The technique is apparent from the very beginning of the cycle, as seen in this extract from the first play, **Kings in Judea**, *broadcast on 21 December 1941.*

SCENE 2 (BETHLEHEM)
SEQUENCE I (*A Shepherd's Cottage*)

THE EVANGELIST: When the wise men had heard King Herod, they departed; and lo! the star, which they saw in the east, went before them, till it came and stood over where the young child was.

SHEPHERD'S WIFE: Zillah, Zillah! Have you laid the table?

ZILLAH: Yes, mother.

WIFE: Then run and tell Father Joseph supper's ready. You'll find him out at the back. And have a look up the road to see if your Dad's coming.

ZILLAH: Yes, Mother. (*She runs out, calling*) Father Joseph, Father Joseph!

WIFE: Now, Mother Mary, let me take the Baby and lay him in the cradle while you have your bit of supper. Come along, lovey, aren't you a beautiful boy, then? There! Now you go off to sleep like a good boy. But he's always wonderful good, ain't he? Never cries hardly at all. Happiest baby as ever I see.

MARY: He is happy in your kind home. But when he was born, he wept.

WIFE: Ah! they all do that, and can you blame them, poor little things, seeing what a cruel hard world it is they come into?

Never mind. We all has our ups and downs. Here's your good
man. Come along, Father Joseph. Here's a nice dish of broiled
meat for you. I'm sure you need it, working so late, too. I
wonder you could see what you were doing.

JOSEPH: It's a grand night. That great white star do shine well-nigh
as bright as the moon – right over the house, seemingly. I've
mended the fence.

WIFE: Isn't it a real bit of luck for us, you being such a fine
carpenter? And so kind, doing all these jobs about the place.

JOSEPH: Well, that's the least I can do, when you've been so
generous and shared your home with us.

WIFE: Well, that was the least *we* could do. We couldn't leave you in
that old stable over in the inn. We'd never a-slept easy in our
beds, knowing there was a mother and baby without no proper
roof to their heads – especially after what Dad told us about
seein' them there angels, and the little boy bein' the blessed
Messiah and all . . . There, Mother Mary, you take and eat that.
It'll do you good . . . D'you think it's really true? About him
bein' the promised Saviour as is to bring back the Kingdom to
Israel?

MARY: I know it is true.

WIFE: How proud you must feel. Don't it seem strange, now, when
you look at him and think about it?

MARY: Sometimes – very strange. I feel as though I were holding the
whole world in my arms – the sky and the sea and the green
earth, and all the seraphim. And then, again, everything
becomes quite simple and familiar, and I know that he is just
my own dear son. If he grew to be wiser than Moses, holier
than Aaron, or more splendid than Solomon, that would still be
true. He will always be my baby, my sweet Jesus, whom I love
– nothing can ever change that.

WIFE: No more it can't; and the queen on her throne can't say no
different. When all's said and done, children are a great
blessing. What's gone with Zillah, I wonder? I hope she ain't
run off too far. There might be wolves about. Hark!

ZILLAH (*running in from outside*): Oh, Mother! Mother!

WIFE: What's up now?

JOSEPH: Hallo, my lass! What's the matter?

ZILLAH: They're coming here! They're coming here! Dad's bringing
them!

WIFE: Who're coming, for goodness' sake?

ZILLAH: Kings – three great kings! riding horseback! They're coming to see the Baby.

WIFE: Kings? Don't talk so soft! Kings, indeed!

ZILLAH: But they *are*. They've got crowns on their heads and rings on their fingers, and servants carrying torches. And they asked Dad, is this where the Baby is? And he said, Yes, and I was to run ahead and say they were coming.

JOSEPH: She's quite right. I can see them from the window. Just turning the corner by the palm-trees.

WIFE: Bless me! and supper not cleared away and everything upside down. Here, mother, let me take your plate. That's better. Zillah, look in the dresser drawer and find a clean bib for Baby Jesus.

ZILLAH: Here you are, Mum . . . One of the kings is a very old gentleman with a long beard and a beautiful scarlet cloak, and the second's all in glittering armour – ooh! and the third's a black man with big gold rings in his ears and the jewels in his turban twinkling like the stars – and his horse is as white as milk, with silver bells on the bridle.

WIFE: Fancy! and all to do honour to our Baby.

JOSEPH: Take heart, Mary. It's all coming true as the Prophet said: The nations shall come to thy light, and kings to the brightness of thy rising.

MARY: Give me my son into my arms.

WIFE: To be sure. He'll set on your knee so brave as a king on his golden throne. Look at him now, the precious lamb . . . Mercy me, here they are.

CASPAR (*at door*): Is this the house?

SHEPHERD (*at door*): Ay, Sirs, this is the house. Pray go in, and ye'll find the Child Jesus wi' his mother.

WIFE: Come in, my lords, come in. Please mind your heads. I fear 'tis but a poor, lowly place.

CASPAR: No place is too lowly to kneel in. There is more holiness here than in King Herod's Temple.

MELCHIOR: More beauty here than in King Herod's palace.

BALTHAZAR: More charity here than in King Herod's heart.

CASPAR: O lady clear as the sun, fair as the moon, the nations of the earth salute your son, the Man born to be King. Hail, Jesus, King of the Jews!

MELCHIOR: Hail, Jesus, King of the World!
BALTHAZAR: Hail, Jesus, King of Heaven!
CASPAR:
MELCHIOR: } All Hail!
BALTHAZAR:

MARY: God bless you, wise old man; and you, tall warrior; and you, dark traveller from desert lands. You come in a strange way, and with a strange message. But that God sent you I am sure, for you and His angels speak with one voice. 'King of the Jews' – why, yes; they told me my son should be the Messiah of Israel. 'King of the World' – that is a very great title; yet when he was born, they proclaimed tidings of joy to all nations. 'King of Heaven' – I don't quite understand that; and yet indeed they said that he should be called the Son of God. You are great and learned men, and I am a very simple woman. What can I say to you, till the time comes when my son can answer for himself?
CASPAR: Alas! the more we know, the less we understand life. Doubts make us afraid to act, and much learning dries the heart. And the riddle that torments the world is this: Shall Wisdom and Love live together at last, when the promised Kingdom comes?
MELCHIOR: We are rulers, and we see that what men need most is good government, with freedom and order. But order puts fetters on freedom, and freedom rebels against order, so that love and power are always at war together. And the riddle that torments the world is this: Shall power and Love dwell together at last, when the promised Kingdom comes?
BALTHAZAR: I speak for a sorrowful people – for the ignorant and the poor. We rise up to labour and lie down to sleep, and night is only a pause between one burden and another. Fear is our daily companion – the fear of want, the fear of war, the fear of cruel death, and of still more cruel life. But all this we could bear if we knew that we did not suffer in vain; that God was beside us in the struggle, sharing the miseries of His own world. For the riddle that torments the world is this: Shall Sorrow and Love be reconciled at last, when the promised Kingdom comes?
MARY: These are very difficult questions – but with me, you see, it is like this. When the Angel's message came to me, the Lord put a song into my heart. I suddenly saw that wealth and cleverness

29

were nothing to God – no one is too unimportant to be His friend. That was the thought that came to me, because of the thing that happened to *me*. I am quite humbly born, yet the Power of God came upon me; very foolish and unlearned, yet the Word of God was spoken to me; and I was in deep distress, when my Baby was born and filled my life with love. So I know very well that Wisdom and Power and Sorrow *can* live together with Love; and for me, the Child in my arms is the answer to all the riddles.

CASPAR: You have spoken a wise word, Mary. Blessed are you among women, and blessed is Jesus your son. Caspar, king of Chaldaea, salutes the King of the Jews with a gift of frankincense.

MELCHIOR: O Mary, you have spoken a word of power. Blessed are you among women, and blessed is Jesus your son. Melchior, King of Pamphylia, salutes the King of the World with a gift of gold.

BALTHAZAR: You have spoken a loving word, Mary, Mother of God. Blessed are you among women, and blessed is Jesus your son. Balthazar, King of Ethiopia, salutes the King of Heaven with a gift of myrrh and spices.

ZILLAH: Oh, look at the great gold crown! Look at the censer all shining with rubies and diamonds, and the blue smoke curling up. How sweet it smells – and the myrrh and aloes, the sweet cloves and the cinnamon. Isn't it lovely? And all for our little Jesus! Let's see which of his presents he likes best. Come, Baby, smile at the pretty crown.

WIFE: Oh, what a solemn, old-fashioned look he gives it.

ZILLAH: He's laughing at the censer—

WIFE: He likes the tinkling of the silver chains.

JOSEPH: He has stretched out his little hand and grasped the bundle of myrrh.

WIFE: Well, there now! You never can tell what they'll take a fancy to.

MARY: Do they not embalm the dead with myrrh? See, now, you sorrowful king, my son has taken your sorrows for his own.

JOSEPH: Myrrh is for love also; as Solomon writes in his Song: A bundle of myrrh is my beloved unto me.

MARY: My lords, we are very grateful to you for all your gifts. And as for the words you have said, be sure that I shall keep all these things and ponder them in my heart.

8

Ballad of the Bread Man

CHARLES CAUSLEY

The Cornish poet Charles Causley often writes in the vigorous, sinewy and colloquial style of the old English ballads, an approach typified by this up-dated version of the birth, life and death of Christ.

Mary stood in the kitchen
Baking a loaf of bread.
An angel flew in through the window.
We've a job for you, he said.

God in his big gold heaven,
Sitting in his big blue chair,
Wanted a mother for his little son.
Suddenly saw you there.

Mary shook and trembled,
It isn't true what you say.
Don't say that, said the angel.
The baby's on its way.

Joseph was in the workshop
Planing a piece of wood.
The old man's past it, the neighbours said.
That girl's been up to no good.

And who was that elegant feller,
They said, in the shiny gear?
The things they said about Gabriel
Were hardly fit to hear.

Mary never answered,
Mary never replied.
She kept the information,
Like the baby, safe inside.

Ballad of the Bread Man

It was election winter.
They went to vote in town.
When Mary found her time had come
The hotels let her down.

The baby was born in an annex
Next to the local pub.
At midnight, a delegation
Turned up from the Farmers' Club.

They talked about an explosion
That cracked a hole in the sky,
Said they'd been sent to the Lamb & Flag
To see god come down from on high.

A few days later a bishop
And a five-star general were seen
With the head of an African country
In a bullet-proof limousine.

We've come, they said, with tokens
For the little boy to choose.
Told the tale about war and peace
In the television news.

After them came the soldiers
With rifle and bomb and gun,
Looking for enemies of the state.
The family had packed and gone.

When they got back to the village
The neighbours said to a man,
That boy will never be one of us,
Though he does what he blessed well can.

He went round to all the people
A paper crown on his head.
Here is some bread from my father.
Take, eat, he said.

Nobody seemed very hungry,
Nobody seemed to care.
Nobody saw the god in himself
Quietly standing there.

Ballad of the Bread Man

He finished up in the papers.
He came to a very bad end.
He was charged with bringing the living to life.
No man was that prisoner's friend.

There's only one kind of punishment
To fit that kind of a crime.
They rigged a trial and shot him dead.
They were only just in time.

They lifted the young man by the leg,
They lifted him by the arm,
They locked him in a cathedral
In case he came to harm.

They stored him safe as water
Under seven rocks.
One Sunday morning he burst out
Like a jack-in-the-box.

Through the town he went walking.
He showed them the holes in his head.
Now do you want any loaves? he cried.
Not today, they said.

9

The Burning Babe

ROBERT SOUTHWELL

Sent abroad in 1576 to study in Douai, Robert Southwell was so inspired by the Jesuit teachers he encountered there that he eventually became a novice, and later a priest, in the Roman Catholic church. He returned to England in 1586, at a time when anti-Catholic feeling was high, and although no direct action was taken against him for some years he was under constant scrutiny by the authorities, which led in the end to his arrest and imprisonment in 1592. He was executed, a martyr to his faith, on 21 February 1595. His poems, preoccupied with religious ideas and imagery, were published soon after: **The Burning Babe** *is perhaps the best known.*

As I in hoary Winter's night stood shiveringe in the snowe,
Surpris'd I was with sodayne heat, which made my hart to
    glowe;
And lifting upp a fearfull eye to vewe what fire was neere,
A pretty Babe all burninge bright, did in the ayre appeare,
Who scorched with excessive heate, such floodes of teares did
    shedd,
As though His floodes should quench His flames which with
    His teares were fedd;
Alas! quoth He, but newly borne, in fiery heates I frye,
Yet none approch to warme their hartes or feele my fire but I!
My faultles brest the fornace is, the fuell woundinge thornes,
Love is the fire, and sighes the smoke, the ashes shame and
    scornes;
The fuell Justice layeth on, and Mercy blowes the coales,
The mettal in this fornace wrought are men's defiled soules,
For which, as nowe on fire I am, to worke them to their goode,
So will I melt into a bath to wash them in My bloode:
With this He vanisht out of sight, and swiftly shroncke awaye,
And straight I called unto mynde that it was Christmas-daye.

The Eve of Christmas

JAMES KIRKUP

James Kirkup has taught in universities in England, France, Sweden, Spain, Malaya and Japan, eventually settling permanently in the latter country as a literary journalist. He is well known as a poet, autobiographer and translator, and has also written novels and plays.

It was the evening before the night
That Jesus turned from dark to light.

Joseph was walking round and round,
And yet he moved not on the ground.

He looked into the heavens, and saw
The pole stood silent, star on star.

He looked into the forest: there
The leaves hung dead upon the air.

He looked into the sea, and found
It frozen, and the lively fishes bound.

And in the sky, the birds that sang
Not in feathered clouds did hang.

Said Joseph: 'What is this silence all?'
An angel spoke: 'It is no thrall,

But is a sign of great delight:
The Prince of Love is born this night.'

And Joseph said: 'Where may I find
This wonder?' – 'He is all mankind,

Look, he is both farthest, nearest,
Highest and lowest, of all men the dearest.'

Then Joseph moved, and found the stars
Moved with him, and the evergreen airs,

The birds went flying, and the main
Flowed with its fishes once again.

And everywhere they went, they cried:
'Love lives, when all had died!'

In Excelsis Gloria!

11

from
The Lore and Language of Schoolchildren

IONA and PETER OPIE

'As well as being a valuable social study, it is one of the most exhilarating anthologies of our day,' said **The Times Literary Supplement** *reviewing* **The Lore and language of Schoolchildren** *by Iona and Peter Opie, when it was first published in 1959. Based on information collected from some 5,000 children in all types of school in England, Scotland and Wales (and one in Dublin), the book is a record of the rhymes, songs, chants, riddles, jokes, catcalls and slang in use by the ordinary schoolchild of that time. Included is a section on beliefs and customs relevant to certain annual festivals, and it is from the section on Christmas that this extract is taken.*

Children's belief in Father Christmas is liable to last until they are six, sometimes longer, and varying notions are entertained about him – Christmas mythology still being in a state of flux. Thus many children are told that he first comes around before Christmas to collect any messages; fairies, pixies, elves . . . and midgets are introduced into the legend as Father Christmas's helpers; and it is not uncommon for children to think that Father Christmas and Santa Claus are two different people. Disbelief in 'Daddy' Christmas comes when parents are spied at night filling the stockings, or when other children disabuse them. An 11-year-old writes:

> 'When I was younger I thought Father Christmas was a wonderful man. On Christmas Eve before I went to bed I would make my mother put out the fire. I was afraid that Father Christmas would get burnt when he climbed down the chimney. My sister would write out my Christmas list (because I couldn't write) and I would throw it up the chimney. When I went to town with my mother, I wondered how Father Christmas could be in all the stores at once. She told me that they were his brothers and the real one came on Christmas Eve. My sister would make a cup of tea and biscuits for him. But when I got to the age of six the older children called me silly because I believed in Father Christmas. When I got home I asked my mother and she said, "Of course there's a Father Christmas," but I did not believe her.'

The custom of leaving refreshment for Father Christmas is particularly common in the north, and its disappearance by the morning is counted additional proof that he really came. In Cumberland Father Christmas is sometimes left a glass of sherry, a cigarette, and half-a-crown. When the girl who said this was asked who got the spoils, she merely grinned, and reiterated that they always had disappeared by morning.

Christmas is everything that can be expected. To children in the south it is '*the* most special day'. 'When I wake up,' says a 9-year-old, 'I say,

> Christmas comes but once a year,
> But when it comes it brings good cheer.'[1]

It is a day of 'undoing presents and taking them round showing them to people'. But all children say it is their stockings they empty first, getting 'hold of the toe and shaking everything out', and leaving the rest of their presents until later. Everybody's house is decorated, and they say they have to wear their best clothes ('which', says a hoyden, 'I do not think is very exciting because you cannot go to play in the fields').

In and around Scarborough the boys go 'Christmas ceshing' (pronounced *Ch'is'mas keshin'*), which requires no equipment beyond a hard fist to knock on doors, and a strong voice to shout – in a special sing-song manner – 'Wish you Merry Christmas, mistress and master'. Their cry can be heard all the way along the street on Christmas morning, and they hope to gain pennies by it.

Some children mention going to church, and that Christmas is 'a day of remembrance for our Lord Jesus Christ'. Rather more children merely speak of the pleasure of hearing church bells on Christmas morning.

One girl (Stoke-on-Trent) says that she goes to a farm and chants:

> Little turkey patter
> Be quick and get much fatter.

Then the farmer brings her back in his car with the turkey. At dinner a turkey or chicken with sausages and stuffing 'smells

---

[1]Thereby echoing the sentiment voiced by Tusser in 1573:
> At Christmas play and make good cheere,
> for Christmas comes but once a yeere.

glorious', so that when a girl sits down to eat she is 'that full in a few minutes' she cannot possibly eat any more.

In the afternoon they listen to the Queen on the wireless, and to Wilfred Pickles at a children's hospital, or – possibly more often – go visiting. At Auntie's 'when you arrive they try to get you under the mistletoe'. 'It is good luck', says a 14-year-old Lloyney girl, 'if the first man to kiss you under the mistletoe gives you a pair of gloves.'

When the evening closes in they usually have a party, inviting their friends to tea and playing 'all kinds of games' such as: The Grand Old Duke of York, The Farmer's in his Den, There was a Jolly Miller, Musical Chairs (or Musical Arms), Blindman's Buff, and Postman's Knock. Children in different parts of Britain name the same games over and over again. Half-way through tea (at Meir in Staffordshire) everyone starts singing:

> Bring out your mince pies,
> Bring out your mince pies,
> And share them all around,
> And share them all around.

And as the evening grows older and merrier they have trifle, nuts, toffees, lemonade, and crackers. The party ends with presents off the Christmas tree 'which is beautifully decorated with crackers and balloons and at the top of the tree there is a lovely fairy'. Sometimes Father Christmas comes to the party. 'My father dressed up as Father Christmas,' says an 11-year-old, 'and then the fun began. Dad came in wearing Mrs. Evans's dressing gown and my hood. He started unloading presents off the tree. My young cousin Stuart who is five asked Dad had he got Rudolph the reindeer with him.[1] Dad said yes. He didn't quite know what to say. Then Stuart and Denise who is three wanted to see him. We told all sorts of things not for them to go out there. Mother had made an excuse for Dad by saying he had gone to Gran's. Then Dad went and as soon as he came back supposedly from Gran's the first thing Stuart told him was "You've missed all the fun, Uncle George. Santa's been here!"'

---

[1]'Rudolph the Red-nosed Reindeer' is the title of a Christmas song.

12

from
Sir Gawain and the Green Knight

*Translation is necessary when presenting extracts from this anonymous fourteenth-century poem, since its language is much more 'foreign' than the comparatively modern vocabulary and sentence structure of the later **Second Shepherds' Pageant**. No attempt has been made to retain the rhyme scheme or the distinctive alliterative pattern of the original poem: the aim has been solely to convey the meaning as easily and simply as possible. The passage is from the beginning of the poem, and describes, in a highly idealized manner, the Christmas celebrations at the court of King Arthur.*

King Arthur lay at Camelot one Christmas
With many loyal lords, his best liegemen,
All those noble brothers of the Round Table.
There was happy revelry and splendid entertainment:
A succession of knights tourneyed and jousted in good-natured
    combat,
Then went off to the court to dance and sing,
For the celebrations went on for fifteen whole days
With all the feasting and merry-making that could be devised.
Such was the great happiness among the lords and ladies in halls
   and chambers
That the sounds of merriment echoed pleasantly by day
With the noise of dancing at night.
With all the joy in the world they passed the time together,
The most famous knights of Christ
And the loveliest ladies that ever lived,
With the most noble king that the court had ever seen.
For the gracious people in that hall were in their prime,
The most blessed on earth;
And their king the most respected in character.
It would be hard to find so noble a company anywhere.

In celebration of the arrival of a brand new year
On New Year's Day, when the king had come into the hall with his
    knights,
Having been to chapel for the singing of mass,
The company on the dais was served double.
A loud cheer was given by priests and laity,
And Christmas was celebrated anew, and named over and over
    again.
Then the lords and ladies hurried to distribute New Year gifts with
    their own hands,

Busily discussing their presents.
Ladies laughed loudly, even though they might have been
    disappointed,
And those who got what they wanted were most certainly not
    annoyed!
This merriment continued until dinner time

When, after they had washed, they took their seats with great
    ceremony,
The most noble at the head of the table, as was fitting.
The fair Queen Guinivere was in their midst,
Sitting on the dais, which was decorated all over,
With fine silk at the sides, a canopy of best Toulouse silk above,
Together with many Turkestan tapestries
Embroidered and set with the best-quality gems that money could
    buy.
Grey-eyed and gracious, no man could deny that she was the fairest
    lady
That had ever been seen.

13

from
The Sword in the Stone

T.H. WHITE

The Arthurian legends have attracted the attention of numerous writers over the centuries, most of them dealing seriously with the stories of knights in armour and the search for the Holy Grail. T.H. White (1906–64), however, took a highly idiosyncratic approach to the life of the young King Arthur in his quartet of novels **The Once and Future King***, and injected a welcome element of humour into the proceedings. Despite the lightness of tone, there is an authentic 'Merry England' feel to this account of Christmas at the Castle of the Forest Sauvage, from* **The Sword in the Stone***, the first of the four.*

It was Christmas night, the eve of the Boxing Day Meet. You must remember that this was in the old Merry England of Gramarye, when the rosy barons ate with their fingers and had peacocks served before them with all their tail feathers streaming, or boars' heads with the tusks stuck in again – when there was no unemployment because there were so few people to be employed – when the forests rang with knights walloping each other on the helm, and the unicorns in the wintry moonlight stamped with their silver feet and snorted their noble breaths of blue upon the frozen air. Such marvels were great and comfortable ones. But in the Old England there was a greater marvel still. The weather behaved itself.

In the spring, the little flowers came out obediently in the meads, and the dew sparkled, and the birds sang. In the summer it was beautifully hot for no less than four months, and, if it did rain just enough for agricultural purposes, they managed to arrange it so that it rained while you were in bed. In the autumn the leaves flamed and rattled before the west winds, tempering their sad adieu with glory. And in the winter, which was confined by statute to two months, the snow lay evenly, three feet thick, but never turned into slush.

It was Christmas night in the Castle of the Forest Sauvage, and all around the castle the snow lay as it ought to lie. It hung heavily on the battlements, like thick icing on a very good cake, and in a few convenient places it modestly turned itself in the clearest icicles of the greatest possible length. It hung on the boughs of the forest trees in rounded lumps, even better than apple-blossom, and occasionally slid off the roofs of the village when it saw the chance of falling on some amusing character and giving pleasure to all. The boys made snowballs with it, but never put stones in them to hurt each other, and the dogs, when they were taken to scombre[1], rolled in it and looked surprised but delighted when they vanished into the bigger drifts. There was skating on the moat, which roared with the gliding bones which they used for skates, while hot chestnuts and spiced mead were served on the bank to all and sundry. The owls hooted. The cooks put out plenty of crumbs for the small birds. The villagers brought out their red mufflers. Sir Ector's face shone redder even than these. And reddest of all shone the cottage fires down the main street of an evening while the winds howled outside and the old English wolves wandered about slavering in an appropriate manner, or sometimes peeping in at the key-holes with their bloody-red eyes.

It was Christmas night and the proper things had been done. The whole village had come to dinner in hall. There had been boar's head and venison and pork and beef and mutton and capons – but no turkey, because this bird had not yet been invented. There had been plum pudding and snap-dragon, with blue fire on the tips of one's fingers, and as much mead as anybody could drink. Sir Ector's health had been drunk with 'Best respects, Measter,' or 'Best compliments of the Season, my lords and ladies, and many of them.' There had been mummers to play an exciting dramatic presentation of a story in which St. George and a Saracen and a funny Doctor did surprising things, also carol-singers who rendered 'Adeste Fideles' and 'I sing of a Maiden', in high, clear, tenor voices. After that, those children who had not been sick from their dinner played Hoodman Blind and other appropriate games, while the young men and maidens danced morris dances in the middle, the tables having been cleared away. The old folks sat round the walls holding glasses of mead in their hands and feeling thankful that they were past such capers, hoppings and skippings, while those children who had been sick sat with them, and soon went to sleep, the small

---

[1]scombre: An obscure word, which presumably means a scamper or run

heads leaning against their shoulders. At the high table Sir Ector sat with his knightly guests, who had come for tomorrow's hunting, smiling and nodding and drinking burgundy or sherris sack or malmsey wine.

The Mummer's Play

The tradition of the Christmas Mummer's Play of St George is a venerable one, stretching back beyond the Middle Ages and surviving well into the present century. It is believed to have evolved from an ancient sword-dance, and in its heyday it was popular throughout the British Isles. Although there were regional differences in the words spoken, the principal characters remained the same, and the action followed a set pattern.

It has been suggested that the central incident of the play was originally connected with the celebration of the death of the old year and its resurrection into a new one.

          [Enter the Presenter]
PRESENTER.   I open the door, I enter in;
        I hope your favour we shall win.
        Stir up the fire and strike a light,
        And see my merry boys act to-night.
        Whether we stand or whether we fall,
        We'll do our best to please you all.

      [Enter the actors, and stand in a clump]
PRESENTER.   Room, room, brave gallants all,
        Pray give us room to rhyme;
        We're come to show activity,
           This merry Christmas time;
        Activity of youth,
        Activity of age,
        The like was never seen
           Upon a common stage.
        And if you don't believe what I say,
        Step in St. George – and clear the way.

[*Enter St. George*]

ST. GEORGE.   In come I, Saint George,
    The man of courage bold;
With my broad axe and sword
    I won a crown of gold.
I fought the fiery dragon,
    And drove him to the slaughter,
And by these means I won
    The King of Egypt's daughter.
Show me the man that bids me stand;
I'll cut him down with my courageous
    hand.

PRESENTER.   Step in, Bold Slasher.

[*Enter Bold Slasher*]

SLASHER.   In come I, the Turkish Knight,
    Come from the Turkish land to fight.
I come to fight St. George,
    The man of courage bold;
And if his blood be hot,
    I soon will make it cold.

ST. GEORGE.   Stand off, stand off, Bold Slasher,
    And let no more be said,
For if I draw my sword,
    I'm sure to break thy head.
Thou speakest very bold,
    To such a man as I;
I'll cut thee into eyelet holes,
    And make thy buttons fly.

SLASHER.   My head is made of iron,
    My body is made of steel,
My arms and legs of beaten brass;
    No man can make me feel.

ST. GEORGE.   Then draw thy sword and fight,
    Or draw thy purse and pay;
For satisfaction I must have,
    Before I go away.

SLASHER.   No satisfaction shalt thou have,
But I will bring thee to thy grave.

ST. GEORGE.   Battle to battle with thee I call,
To see who on this ground shall fall.

SLASHER.   Battle to battle with thee I pray,
To see who on this ground shall lay.

ST. GEORGE.   Then guard thy body and mind
thy head,
Or else my sword shall strike thee dead.

SLASHER.   One shall die and the other shall live;
This is the challenge that I do give.

[*They fight. Slasher falls*]

from
Fantastickes

NICHOLAS BRETON

Nicholas Breton's work spans the Elizabethan and Jacobean periods, and is contemporary with that of William Shakespeare. One of the innumerable minor writers which this fertile period engendered, Breton seems to have specialized in sharply-observed sketches of people, customs and activities of his time; his account of an early seventeenth-century Christmas is taken from his collection entitled **Fantastickes***, published in 1626.*

It is now Christmas, and not a cup of drink must pass without a carol; the beasts, fowl, and fish, come to a general execution; and the corn is ground to dust for the bakehouse, and the pastry. Cards and dice purge many a purse, and the youth shew their agility in shoeing of the wild mare. Now 'Good cheer', and 'Welcome', and 'God be with you', and 'I thank you', and 'Against the new year', provide for the presents. The Lord of Misrule is no mean man for his time, and the guests of the high table must lack no wine. The lusty bloods must look about them like men, and piping and dancing puts away much melancholy. Stolen venison is sweet, and a fat coney is worth money. Pit-falls are now set for small birds, and a woodcock hangs himself in a gin. A good fire heats all the house, and a full alms-basket makes the beggars' prayers. The masquers and mummers make the merry sport; but if they lose their money, their drum goes dead. Swearers and swaggerers are sent away to the ale-house, and unruly wenches go in danger of judgement. Musicians now make their instruments speak out, and a good song is worth the hearing. In sum, it is a holy time, a duty in Christians for the remembrance of Christ, and custom among friends for the maintenance of good fellowship. In brief, I thus conclude of it: I hold it a memory of the Heaven's love and the world's peace, the mirth of the honest, and the meeting of the friendly.

from
The Diary of Samuel Pepys

It is as the author of the famous Diary that Samuel Pepys is best remembered. He was, however, primarily a civil servant, and a figure of some importance in the political life of his time: beginning as a clerk within the Exchequer, he advanced to the position of Surveyor General of the naval victualling office and was spectacularly successful in regenerating the country's fleet, an achievement acknowledged by the historian Sir Arthur Bryant in the subtitle of one volume of his biography of Pepys, **The Saviour of the Navy.***

The Diary itself, written in shorthand, was started in 1659 and continued until mid-1667, covering therefore such stirring events as the Plague and the Great Fire of London. After Pepys's death in 1703 the manuscript was left to a nephew and later to Pepys's old college, Magdalene College, Cambridge. The text was not transcribed for publication until 1819, and the task took some three years to complete. The extracts presented here, a selection of three Christmas entries, show Pepys as a wry observer of human nature.

Dec. 25, 1662 Christmas Day.   Had a pleasant walk to White Hall, where I intended to have received the communion with the family, but I come a little too late. So I walked up into the house, and spent my time looking over pictures, particularly the ships in King Henry the VIIIth's voyage to Boulogne; marking the great difference between those built then and now. By and by down to the chapel again, where Bishop Morley preached upon the song of the Angels, 'Glory to God on high, on earth peace, and good will towards men.' Methought he made but a poor sermon, but long, and, reprehending the common jollity of the Court for the true joy that shall and ought to be on these days, particularized concerning their excesse in playes and gaming, saying that he whose office it is to keep the gamesters in order and within bounds, serves but for a second rather in a duell, meaning the groome-porter. Upon which it was worth observing how far they are come from taking the reprehensions of a bishop seriously, that they all laugh in the chapel when he reflected on their ill actions and courses. He did much press us to

49

joy in these public days of joy, and to hospitality. But one that stood by whispered in my eare that the Bishop do not spend one groate to the poor himself. The sermon done, a good anthem followed with viols, and the King come down to receive the Sacrament.

1665 Christmas day. To church in the morning, and there saw a wedding in the church, which I have not seen many a day; and the young people so merry with one another! and strange to say what delight we married people have to see these poor fools decoyed into our condition, every man and woman gazing and smiling at them.

1668 Christmas-day. To dinner alone with my wife, who, poor wretch! sat undressed all day, till ten at night, altering and lacing of a noble petticoat: while I by her, making the boy read to me the life of Julius Caesar, and Des Cartes, book of Musick.
28th. Called up by drums and trumpets; these things and boxes[1] having cost me much money this Christmas already, and will do more.

---

[1]boxes: presents

from
A Christmas Carol

CHARLES DICKENS

For many people the perfect example of a Christmas story is Charles Dickens'
***A Christmas Carol** (1843), and the character of Ebenezer Scrooge must be familiar*
even to those who have never actually read the book. 'May [the story] haunt their
houses pleasantly,' wrote Dickens in the short Preface, and this it has continued to
do for 140 years, with new television, stage or radio adaptations appearing
frequently as each Christmas approaches. Since the story is so much a part of our
general consciousness, two extracts have been chosen: the first describes the way in
which the Cratchits, in spite of their poverty, celebrate Christmas in a happy and
generous spirit, and the second, from the end of the book, shows how Scrooge
himself, after his ghostly experiences, learns the true meaning of 'goodwill to all
men', and immediately puts it into practice.

Such a bustle ensued that you might have thought a goose the
rarest of all birds; a feathered phenomenon, to which a black swan
was a matter of course – and in truth it was something very like it in
that house. Mrs. Cratchit made the gravy (ready beforehand in a
little saucepan) hissing hot; Master Peter mashed the potatoes with
incredible vigour; Miss Belinda sweetened up the apple-sauce;
Martha dusted the hot plates; Bob took Tiny Tim beside him in a
tiny corner at the table; the two young Cratchits set chairs for
everybody, not forgetting themselves, and mounting guard upon
their posts, crammed spoons into their mouths, lest they should
shriek for goose before their turn came to be helped. At last the
dishes were set on, and grace was said. It was succeeded by a
breathless pause, as Mrs. Cratchit, looking slowly all along the
carving-knife, prepared to plunge it in the breast; but when she
did, and when the long expected gush of stuffing issued forth, one
murmur of delight arose all round the board, and even Tiny Tim,
excited by the two young Cratchits, beat on the table with the
handle of his knife, and feebly cried Hurrah!

There never was such a goose. Bob said he didn't believe there ever was such a goose cooked. Its tenderness and flavour, size and cheapness, were the themes of universal admiration. Eked out by apple-sauce and mashed potatoes, it was sufficient dinner for the whole family; indeed, as Mrs. Cratchit said with great delight (surveying one small atom of a bone upon the dish), they hadn't ate it all at last! Yet every one had had enough, and the youngest Cratchits in particular, were steeped in sage and onion to the eyebrows! But now, the plates being changed by Miss Belinda, Mrs. Cratchit left the room alone – too nervous to bear witnesses – to take the pudding up and bring it in.

Suppose it should not be done enough! Suppose it should break in turning out! Suppose somebody should have got over the wall of the back-yard, and stolen it, while they were merry with the goose – a supposition at which the two young Cratchits became livid! All sorts of horrors were supposed.

Hallo! A great deal of steam! The pudding was out of the copper. A smell like a washing-day! That was the cloth. A smell like an eating-house and a pastrycook's next door to each other, with a laundress's next door to that! That was the pudding! In half a minute Mrs. Cratchit entered – flushed, but smiling proudly – with the pudding, like a speckled cannon-ball, so hard and firm, blazing in half of half-a-quartern of ignited brandy, and bedight with Christmas holly stuck into the top.

Oh, a wonderful pudding! Bob Cratchit said, and calmly too, that he regarded it as the greatest success achieved by Mrs Cratchit since their marriage. Mrs. Cratchit said that now the weight was off her mind, she would confess she had had her doubts about the quantity of flour. Everybody had something to say about it, but nobody said or thought it was at all a small pudding for a large family. It would have been flat heresy to do so. Any Cratchit would have blushed to hint at such a thing.

At last the dinner was all done, the cloth was cleared, the hearth swept, and the fire made up. The compound in the jug being tasted, and considered perfect, apples and oranges were put upon the table, and a shovel-full of chestnuts on the fire. Then all the Cratchit family drew round the hearth, in what Bob Cratchit called a circle, meaning half a one; and at Bob Cratchit's elbow stood the family display of glass. Two tumblers, and a custard-cup without a handle.

These held the hot stuff from the jug, however, as well as golden goblets would have done; and Bob served it out with beaming looks, while the chestnuts on the fire sputtered and cracked noisily. Then Bob proposed:

'A Merry Christmas to us all, my dears. God bless us!'

Which all the family re-echoed.

* * * *

He went to church, and walked about the streets, and watched the people hurrying to and fro, and patted children on the head and questioned beggars, and looked down into the kitchens of houses, and up to the windows, and found that everything could yield him pleasure. He had never dreamed that any walk – that anything – could give him so much happiness. In the afternoon he turned his steps towards his nephew's house.

'Is your master at home, my dear?' said Scrooge to the girl.

'He's in the dining-room, sir, along with the mistress. I'll show you upstairs, if you please.'

'Thank'ee. He knows me,' said Scrooge, with his hand already on the dining-room lock. 'I'll go in here, my dear.'

'Why bless my soul!' cried Fred, 'who's that?'

'It's I. Your uncle Scrooge. I have come to dinner. Will you let me in, Fred?'

Let him in! It's a mercy he didn't shake his arm off. He was at home in five minutes. Nothing could be heartier. His niece looked just the same. So did Topper when *he* came. So did the plump sister when *she* came. So did every one when they came. Wonderful party, wonderful games, wonderful unanimity, wonderful happiness!

But he was early at the office next morning. Oh, he was early there. If only he could be there first, and catch Bob Cratchit coming late! That was the thing he had set his heart on.

And he did it; yes, he did! The clock struck nine. No Bob. A quarter past. No Bob. He was full eighteen minutes and a half behind his time. Scrooge sat with his door wide open, that he might see him coming into the office. His hat was off, before he opened the door; his comforter too. He was on his stool in a jiffy; driving away with his pen, as if he were trying to overtake nine o'clock.

'Hallo!' growled Scrooge, in his accustomed voice, as near as he could feign it. 'What do you mean by coming here at this time of day?'

'I am very sorry, sir,' said Bob. 'I *am* behind my time.'

'You are?' repeated Scrooge. 'Yes. I think you are. Step this way, sir, if you please.'

'It's only once a year, sir,' pleaded Bob, appearing from the office. 'It shall not be repeated. I was making rather merry yesterday, sir.'

'Now, I'll tell you what, my friend,' said Scrooge, 'I am not going to stand this sort of thing any longer. And therefore,' he continued, leaping from his stool, and giving Bob such a dig in the waistcoat that he staggered back into the office again; 'and therefore I am about to raise your salary! A merry Christmas, Bob!' said Scrooge, with an earnestness that could not be mistaken, as he clapped him on the back. 'A merrier Christmas, Bob, my good fellow, than I have given you for many a year! I'll raise your salary, and endeavour to assist your struggling family, and we will discuss your affairs this very afternoon, over a Christmas bowl of smoking bishop, Bob! Make up the fires, and buy another coal-scuttle before you dot another i, Bob Cratchit!'

from
The Pickwick Papers

by CHARLES DICKENS

Dickens' first full-length novel described the picaresque adventures of Mr Pickwick and his companions, which were serialized in monthly magazine instalments beginning in March 1836. The December edition offered obvious opportunities to bring a seasonal twist to the story, and accordingly Chapter 36 of **The Pickwick Papers**, *'A Good-humoured Christmas Chapter', finds Mr Pickwick spending the festive season at Mr Wardle's house in Dingley Dell: the Christmas party is described with that rather naïve sentimentality characteristic of Dickens' early work.*

From the centre of the ceiling of this kitchen, old Wardle had just suspended with his own hands a huge branch of mistletoe, and this same branch of mistletoe instantaneously gave rise to a scene of general and most delightful struggling and confusion; in the midst of which Mr. Pickwick with a gallantry which would have done honour to a descendant of Lady Tollimglower herself, took the old lady by the hand, led her beneath the mystic branch, and saluted her in all courtesy and decorum. The old lady submitted to this piece of practical politeness with all the dignity which befitted so important and serious a solemnity, but the younger ladies, not being so thoroughly imbued with a superstitious veneration of the custom, or imagining that the value of a salute is very much enhanced if it cost a little trouble to obtain it, screamed and struggled, and ran into corners, and threatened and remonstrated, and did everything but leave the room, until some of the less adventurous gentlemen were on the point of desisting, when they all at once found it useless to resist any longer, and submitted to be kissed with a good grace. Mr. Winkle kissed the young lady with the black eyes, and Mr. Snodgrass kissed Emily; and Mr. Weller, not being particular about the form of being under the mistletoe, kissed Emma and the other female servants, just as he caught them. As to the poor relations, they kissed everybody, not even excepting the plainer portion of the young-lady visitors, who, in their excessive confusion, ran right under the mistletoe, directly it was hung up, without knowing it! Wardle stood with his back to the fire, surveying the whole scene, with the utmost satisfaction; and the fat boy took the opportunity of appropriating to his own use, and summarily devouring, a particularly fine mince-pie, that had been carefully put by, for somebody else.

Now the screaming had subsided, and faces were in a glow and curls in a tangle, and Mr. Pickwick, after kissing the old lady as before-mentioned, was standing under the mistletoe, looking with a very pleased countenance on all that was passing around him, when the young lady with the black eyes, after a little whispering with the other young ladies, made a sudden dart forward, and, putting her arm round Mr. Pickwick's neck, saluted him affectionately on the left cheek; and before Mr. Pickwick distinctly knew what was the matter, he was surrounded by the whole body, and kissed by every one of them.

It was a pleasant thing to see Mr. Pickwick in the centre of the group, now pulled this way, and then that, and first kissed on the chin and then on the nose, and then on the spectacles, and to hear the peals of laughter which were raised on every side; but it was a still more pleasant thing to see Mr. Pickwick, blinded shortly afterwards, with a silk-handkerchief, falling up against the wall, and scrambling into corners, and going through all the mysteries of blind-man's buff, with the utmost relish for the game, until at last he caught one of the poor relations; and then had to evade the blind man himself, which he did with a nimbleness and agility that elicited the admiration and applause of all beholders. The poor relations caught just the people whom they thought would like it; and when the game flagged, got caught themselves. When they were all tired of blind-man's buff, there was a great game at snapdragon, and when fingers enough were burned with that, and all the raisins gone, they sat down by the huge fire of blazing logs to a substantial supper, and a mighty bowl of wassail, something smaller than an ordinary washhouse copper, in which the hot apples were hissing and bubbling with a rich look, and a jolly sound, that were perfectly irresistible.

'This,' said Mr. Pickwick, looking round him, 'this is, indeed, comfort.'

from
Our Village

MARY RUSSELL MITFORD

In the Preface to **Our Village**, *published in 1848, Miss Mitford explains that in her book she had made 'an attempt to delineate country scenery and country manners, as they exist in a small village in the south of England . . . Her descriptions have always been written on the spot, and at the moment, and in nearly every instance with the closest and most resolute fidelity to the places and the people.'*

The chapter from which this extract is taken describes the preparations for a Christmas party made by the proprietress of the local inn, Hester Frost, who has some very firm ideas of how things are to be organised. She insists to her husband Jacob, a travelling fruit and fish salesman, that there will be no mistletoe boughs, on the grounds that their presence is conducive to immorality; that an attractive widow, Mrs Glen, will not be included on the guest list; and that one of the village's well-known characters, old Timothy, will not be invited because of his tendency to get drunk very quickly. Although Jacob apparently agrees to all this, Hester has not been married to him long enough to know that he has his own way of doing things . . .

Of the unrest of that week of bustling preparation, words can give but a faint image – Oh, the scourings, the cleanings, the sandings, the dustings, the scoldings of that disastrous week! The lame ostler and the red-haired parish girl were worked off their feet – 'even Sunday shone no Sabbath-day to them' – for then did the lame ostler trudge eight miles to the church of a neighbouring parish, to procure the attendance of a celebrated bassoon player to officiate in lieu of Timothy; whilst the poor little maid was sent nearly as far to the next town, in quest of an itinerant show-woman, of whom report had spoken at the Bell, to beat the tambourine. The show-woman proved undiscoverable; but the bassoon player having promised to come, and to bring with him a clarionet, Mrs. Frost was at ease as to her music; and having provided more victuals than the whole village could have discussed at a sitting, and having moreover adorned her house with berried holly, china-roses, and chrysanthemums, after the most tasteful manner, began to enter

57

into the spirit of the thing, and to wish for the return of her husband, to admire and to praise.

Late on the great day Jacob arrived, his cart laden with marine stores for his share of the festival. Never had our goodly village witnessed such a display of oysters, muscles, perriwinkles, and cockles, to say nothing of apples and nuts, and two little kegs, snugly covered up, which looked exceedingly as if they had cheated the revenue, a packet of green tea, which had something of the same air, and a new silk gown, of a flaming salmon-colour, straight from Paris, which he insisted on Hester's retiring to assume, whilst he remained to arrange the table and receive the company, who, it being now about four o'clock p.m. – our good rustics can never have enough of a good thing – were beginning to assemble for the ball.

The afternoon was fair and cold, and dry and frosty, and Matthewses, Bridgwaters, Whites, and Joneses, in short the whole farmerage and shopkeepery of the place, with a goodly proportion of wives and daughters, came pouring in apace. Jacob received them with much gallantry, uncloaking and unbonneting the ladies, assisted by his two staring and awkward auxiliaries, welcoming their husbands and fathers, and apologizing, as best he might, for the absence of his helpmate; who, 'perplexed in the extreme' by her new finery, which happening to button down the back, she was fain to put on hind side before, did not make her appearance till the greater part of the company had arrived, and the music had struck up a country dance. An evil moment, alas! did poor Hester choose for her entry! For the first sound that met her ear was Timothy's fiddle, forming a strange trio with the bassoon and the clarionet: and the first persons whom she saw were Tom Higgs cracking walnuts at the chimney-side, and Sandy Frazer saluting the widow Glen under the mistletoe. How she survived such sights and sounds does appear wonderful – but survive them she did – for at three o'clock, a.m., when our reporter left the party, she was engaged in a social game at cards, which, by the description, seems to have been long whist, with the identical widow Glen, Sandy Frazer, and William Ford, and had actually won fivepence-halfpenny of Martha's money; the young folks were still dancing gaily, to the sound of Timothy's fiddle, which fiddle had the good quality of going on almost as well drunk as sober, and it was now playing solo, the clarionet being *hors-de-combat* and the bassoon under the table. Tom Higgs, after showing off more tricks than a monkey, amongst the rest sewing the whole card-party together by the skirts, to the probable damage of Mrs. Frost's gay gown, had returned to his old post by the fire, and his old amusement of cracking walnuts, with the shells of which he was pelting the little parish girl, who sat fast asleep on the other side; and Jacob Frost in all his glory, sat in a cloud of tobacco smoke, roaring out catches with his old friend George Bridgwater, and half a dozen other 'drowthy cronies,' whilst 'aye the ale was growing better,' and the Christmas party went merrily on.

from
The Journal of Ellen Buxton, 1861

Among the accomplishments expected of a well-brought up and respectable Victorian girl, such as painting in water-colours, playing the piano and singing, was the keeping of a journal or diary. The Journal of Ellen Buxton, born in 1848, is one such document, chronicling in a naïve and charming way the everyday events in a upper middle-class family of the 1860s. This extract, from Christmas 1861, is of interest for its social detail: the obligatory charity visit to the poor, and the Victorian family gathering at which an hour and a half spent in listening to children's recitations was considered not at all excessive.

Monday, December 23   This afternoon we went to the Almshouses near here and gave to each of the people half a pound of tea and a pound of sugar, which they liked very much.

Wednesday, December 25   Christmas Day. Last night, we filled Timmie's, Alfred's, Janet's and Barclay's stockings with some little presents, and so when they went to put on their stockings this morning they found all the things and were very much pleased with them. We went to Church this morning at eleven and saw the Church all nicely decorated with evergreens. In the afternoon at two o'clock we all had a nice walk . . . in the forest, and about four we all separated and went home.

On Christmas Day in the evening Papa, Arthur, Lisa, Geoffrey and I went to say our Christmas pieces at Aunt Barclay's. Every year we all of us learn a piece of poetry to say at Christmas, so this year we all went in the carriage and said them at Aunt Barclay's; they were all very pretty pieces and very nicely said; it took just an hour and a half to say them all. At half past six we had a beautiful dinner with two turkeys, because one was not enough; we also had a plum pudding on fire. After dinner we played games and went away about 8.

21

A Royal Christmas

After the death of Prince Albert in 1861, Queen Victoria spent most of her Christmases at Osborne House, on the Isle of Wight, where, as a contemporary writer, W.F. Dawson noted, she enjoyed 'the society of her children and grandchildren, who meet together as less exalted families do at this merry season to reciprocate the same homely delights as those which are experienced throughout the land'.

The 'less exalted families' of the workers and servants of the Osborne estate were not forgotten by the Queen at this time of the year, and the following extract by an anonymous magazine writer describes with deferential enthusiasm the seasonal exercise of regal charity.

This afternoon a pleasant little festivity has been celebrated at Osborne House, where her Majesty, with an ever-kindly interest in her servants and dependants, has for many years inaugurated Christmas in a similar way, the children of her tenantry and the old and infirm enjoying by the Royal bounty the first taste of Christmas fare. The Osborne estate now comprises 5,000 acres, and it includes the Prince Consort's model farm. The children of the labourers – who are housed in excellent cottages – attend the Whippingham National Schools, a pretty block of buildings, distant one mile from Osborne. About half the number of scholars live upon the Queen's estate, and, in accordance with annual custom, the mistresses of the schools, the Misses Thomas, accompanied by the staff of teachers, have conducted a little band of boys and girls – fifty-four in all – to the house, there to take tea and to receive the customary Christmas gifts. Until very recently the Queen herself presided at the distribution; but the Princess Beatrice has lately relieved her mother of the fatigue involved; for the ceremony is no mere formality, it is made the occasion of many a kindly word the remembrance of which far outlasts the gifts. All sorts of rumours are current on the estate for weeks before this Christmas Eve gathering as to the nature of the presents to be bestowed, for no one is supposed to know beforehand what they will be; but there was a pretty shrewd guess to-day that the boys would be given gloves, and the girls cloaks. In some cases the former had had scarves or cloth for suits, and the latter dresses or shawls. Whatever the Christmas presents may be, here they are, arranged upon tables in two long lines, in the servants' hall. To this holly-decorated apartment the expectant youngsters are brought, and their delighted gaze falls upon a huge Christmas-tree laden with beautiful toys. Everybody knows that the tree will be there, and moreover that its summit will be crowned with a splendid doll. Now, the ultimate ownership of this doll is a matter of much concern; it needs deliberation, as it is awarded to the best child, and the judges are the children themselves. The trophy is handed to the keeping of Miss Thomas, and on the next 1st of May the children select by their votes the most popular girl in the school to be elected May Queen. To her the gift goes, and no fairer way could be devised. The Princess Beatrice always makes a point of knowing to whom the prize has been awarded. Her Royal Highness is so constantly a visitor to the cottagers and to the school that she has many an inquiry to make of the little ones as they come forward to receive their gifts.

The girls are called up first by the mistress, and Mr. Andrew Blake, the steward, introduces each child to the Princess Beatrice, to whom Mr Blake hands the presents that her Royal Highness may bestow them upon the recipients with a word of good will, which makes the day memorable. Then the boys are summoned to participate in the distribution of good things, which, it should be explained, consist not only of seasonable and sensible clothing, but toys from the tree, presented by the Queen's grandchildren, who, with their parents, grace the ceremony with their presence and make the occasion one of family interest. The Ladies-in-Waiting also attend. Each boy and girl gets in addition a nicely-bound story-book and a large slice of plum pudding neatly packed in paper, and if any little one is sick at home its portion is carefully reserved. But the hospitality of the Queen is not limited to the children. On alternate years the old men and women resident on the estate are given, under the same pleasant auspices, presents of blankets or clothing. To-day it was the turn of the men, and they received tweed for suits. The aged people have their pudding as well. For the farm labourers and boys, who are not bidden to this entertainment, there is a distribution of tickets, each representing a goodly joint of beef for the Christmas dinner. The festivity this afternoon was brought to a close by the children singing the National Anthem in the courtyard.

from
Kilvert's Diary

*The Rev. Francis Kilvert kept his diary between 1870 and 1879, and in it reveals himself as a fine example of the muscular Christianity, **Boys' Own Paper**, cold-shower philosopher. A devotee of sea bathing in the nude, he became on one occasion very annoyed at the 'detestable custom' of wearing a bathing-costume in the interests of decency; this, he felt, took away all the 'delicious feeling of freedom in stripping in the open air and running down naked to the sands where the waves were curling white with foam . . .' The same brisk fortitude in the face of cold water is found in the first diary extract, written from his own parish at Clyro in Wales. By the time of the second entry, a few days later, he had gone to spend some time with his parents in Wiltshire.*

Sunday, Christmas Day 1870   As I lay awake praying in the early morning I thought I heard a sound of distant bells. It was an intense frost. I sat down in my bath upon a sheet of thick ice which broke in the middle into large pieces whilst sharp points and jagged edges stuck all around the sides of the tub like *chevaux de frise*, not particularly comfortable to the naked thighs and loins, for the keen ice cut like broken glass. The ice water stung and scorched like fire. I had to collect the frozen pieces of ice and pile them on a chair before I could use the sponge and then I had to thaw the sponge in my hands for it was a mass of ice. The morning was brilliant. Walked to the Sunday School with Gibbins and the road sparkled with millions of rainbows, the seven colours gleaming in every glittering point of hoar frost. The church was very cold in spite of two roaring stove fires.

Wednesday, 28 December.   An inch of snow fell last night and as we walked to Draycot to skate the storm began again. As we passed Langley Burrell Church we heard the strains of the quadrille band on the ice at Draycot. The afternoon grew murky and when we began to skate the air was thick with falling snow. But it soon stopped and gangs of labourers were at work immediately sweeping away the new fallen snow . . . The Lancers was beautifully skated. When it grew dark the ice was lighted with Chinese lanterns, and the intense glare of blue, green and crimson lights and magnesium riband made the whole place as light as day. Then people skated with torches.

23

from
Under the Greenwood Tree

THOMAS HARDY

Under the Greenwood Tree (1872) was one of Hardy's earliest novels, and is full of quiet humour and a delight in the old ways of the countryside. This is exemplified in the extract, which concerns the Mellstock choir on its annual carol-singing tour of the village, conscientiously making the rounds of their area but on this occasion rather uncertain of the reception they may be given by the village's new school-teacher, Fancy Day. Here are affectionately portrayed the opinions of country people who are staunch upholders of things as they have always been, and who will have nothing to do with new-fangled ideas and notions.

Mellstock was a parish of considerable acreage, the hamlets composing it lying at a much greater distance from each other than is ordinarily the case. Hence several hours were consumed in playing and singing within hearing of every family, even if but a single air were bestowed on each. There was Lower Mellstock, the main village; half a mile from this were the church and vicarage, and a few other houses, the spot being rather lonely now, though in past centuries it had been the most thickly-populated quarter of the parish. A mile north-east lay the hamlet of Upper Mellstock, where the tranter lived; and at other points knots of cottages, besides solitary farmsteads and dairies.

Old William Dewy, with the violoncello, played the bass; his grandson Dick the treble violin; and Reuben and Michael Mail the tenor and second violins respectively. The singers consisted of four men and seven boys, upon whom devolved the task of carrying and attending to the lanterns, and holding the books open for the players. Directly music was the theme, old William ever and instinctively came to the front.

'Now mind, neighbours,' he said, as they all went out one by one at the door, he himself holding it ajar and regarding them with a critical face as they passed, like a shepherd counting out his sheep. 'You two counter-boys, keep your ears open to Michael's fingering, and don't ye go straying into the treble part along o' Dick and his set, as ye did last year; and mind this especially when we be in "Arise, and hail." Billy Chimlen, don't you sing quite so raving mad as you fain would; and, all o' ye, whatever ye do, keep from making a great scuffle on the ground when we go in to people's gates; but go quietly, so as to strike up all of a sudden, like spirits.'

'Farmer Ledlow's first?'

'Farmer Ledlow's first; the rest as usual.'

'And, Voss,' said the tranter terminatively, 'you keep house here till about half-past two; then heat the metheglin and cider in the warmer you'll find turned up upon the copper; and bring it wi' the victuals to church-hatch, as th'st know.'

Just before the clock struck twelve they lighted the lanterns and started. The moon, in her third quarter, had risen since the snow-storm; but the dense accumulation of snow-cloud weakened her power to a faint twilight, which was rather pervasive of the land-scape than traceable to the sky. The breeze had gone down, and the rustle of their feet and tones of their speech echoed with an alert rebound from every post, boundary-stone, and ancient wall they passed, even where the distance of the echo's origin was less than a few yards. Beyond their own slight noises nothing was to be heard, save the occasional bark of foxes in the direction of Yalbury Wood, or the brush of a rabbit among the grass now and then, as it scampered out of their way.

Most of the outlying homesteads and hamlets had been visited by about two o'clock; they then passed across the outskirts of a wooded park toward the main village, nobody being at home at the Manor. Pursuing no recognized track, great care was necessary in walking lest their faces should come in contact with the low-hanging boughs of the old lime-trees, which in many spots formed dense over-growths of interlaced branches.

'Times have changed from the times they used to be,' said Mail, regarding nobody can tell what interesting old panoramas with an inward eye, and letting his outward glance rest on the ground, because it was as convenient a position as any. 'People don't care much about us now! I've been thinking we must be almost the last left in the county of the old string players? Barrel-organs, and the things next door to 'em that you blow wi' your foot, have come in terribly of late years.'

'Ay!' said Bowman, shaking his head; and old William, on seeing him, did the same thing.

'More's the pity,' replied another. 'Time was – long and merry ago now! – when not one of the varmits was to be heard of; but it served some of the quires right. They should have stuck to strings as we did, and kept out clarinets, and done away with serpents.[1] If you'd thrive in musical religion, stick to strings, says I.'

'Strings be safe soul-lifters, as far as that do go,' said Mr. Spinks.

'Yet there's worse things than serpents,' said Mr. Penny. 'Old things pass away, 'tis true; but a serpent was a good old note: a deep rich note was the serpent.'

'Clar'nets, however, be bad at all times,' said Michael Mail. 'One Christmas – years agone now, years – I went the rounds wi' the Weatherbury quire. 'Twas a hard frosty night, and the keys of all the clar'nets froze – ah, they did freeze! – so that 'twas like drawing a cork every time a key was opened; and the players o' 'em had to go into a hedger-and-ditcher's chimley-corner, and thaw their clar'nets every now and then. An icicle o' spet hung down from the end of every man's clar'net a span long; and as to fingers – well, there, if ye'll believe me, we had no fingers at all, to our knowing.'

'I can well bring back to my mind,' said Mr. Penny, 'what I said to poor Joseph Ryme (who took the treble part in Chalk-Newton Church for two-and-forty year) when they thought of having clar'nets there. "Joseph," I said, says I, "depend upon't, if so be you have them tooting clar'nets you'll spoil the whole set-out. Clar'nets were not made for the service of the Lard; you can see it by looking at 'em," I said. And what came o't? Why, souls, the parson set up a barrel-organ on his own account within two years o' the time I spoke, and the old quire went to nothing.'

'As far as look is concerned,' said the tranter, 'I don't for my part see that a fiddle is much nearer heaven than a clar'net. 'Tis further off. There's always a rakish, scampish twist about a fiddle's looks that seems to say the Wicked One had a hand in making o' en; while angels be supposed to play clar'nets in heaven, or som'at like 'em, if ye may believe picters.'

'Robert Penny, you was in the right,' broke in the eldest Dewy. 'They should ha' stuck to strings. Your brass man is a rafting dog[2] –

---

[1]Serpent: a bass instrument made of wood and formed by three U-shaped turns.
[2]Rafting dog: a vigorous performer.

well and good; your reed-man is a dab at stirring ye – well and good; your drum-man is a rare bowel-shaker – good again. But I don't care who hears me say it, nothing will spak to your heart wi' the sweetness o' the man of strings!'

'Strings for ever!' said little Jimmy.

'Strings alone would have held their ground against all the new comers in creation.' ('True, true!' said Bowman.) 'But clarinets was death.' ('Death they was!' said Mr. Penny.) 'And harmonions,' William continued in a louder voice, and getting excited by these signs of approval, 'harmonions and barrel-organs' ('Ah!' and groans from Spinks) 'to be miserable – what shall I call 'em? – miserable –'

'Sinners,' suggested Jimmy, who made large strides like the men, and did not lag behind like the other little boys.

'Miserable dumbledores!'[1]

'Right, William, and so they be – miserable dumbledores!' said the choir with unanimity.

By this time they were crossing to a gate in the direction of the school, which, standing on a slight eminence at the junction of three ways, now rose in unvarying and dark flatness against the sky. The instruments were returned, and all the band entered the school enclosure, enjoined by old William to keep upon the grass.

'Number seventy-eight,' he softly gave out as they formed round in a semicircle, the boys opening the lanterns to get a clearer light, and directing their rays on the books.

Then passed forth into the quiet night an ancient and time-worn hymn, embodying a quaint Christianity in words orally transmitted from father to son through several generations down to the present characters, who sang them out right earnestly:

> 'Remember Adam's fall,
>   O thou Man:
> Remember Adam's fall
>   From Heaven to Hell.
> Remember Adam's fall;
>   How he hath condemn'd all
> In Hell perpetual
>   There for to dwell.

---

[1] bumblebees.

Remember God's goodnesse,
  O thou Man:
Remember God's goodnesse,
  His promise made.
Remember God's goodnesse;
He sent His Son sinlesse
Our ails for to redress;
  Be not afraid!

In Bethlehem He was born,
  O thou Man:
In Bethlehem He was born,
  For mankind's sake.
In Bethlehem He was born,
Christmas-day i' the morn:
Our Saviour thought no scorn
  Our faults to take.

Give thanks to God alway,
  O thou Man:
Give thanks to God alway
  With heart-most joy.
Give thanks to God alway
On this our joyful day:
Let all men sing and say,
  Holy, Holy!'

Having concluded the last note, they listened for a minute or two, but found that no sound issued from the schoolhouse.

'Four breaths, and then, "O, what unbounded goodness!" number fifty-nine,' said William.

This was duly gone through, and no notice whatever seemed to be taken of the performance.

'Good guide us, surely 'tisn't a' empty house, as befell us in the year thirty-nine and forty-three!' said old Dewy.

'Perhaps she's jist come from some musical city, and sneers at our doings?' the tranter whispered.

''Od rabbit her!' said Mr. Penny, with an annihilating look at a corner of the school chimney, 'I don't quite stomach her, if this is it. Your plain music well done is as worthy as your other sort done bad, a' b'lieve, souls; so say I.'

'Four breaths, and then the last,' said the leader authoritatively. '"Rejoice, ye Tenants of the Earth," number sixty-four.'

At the close, waiting yet another minute, he said in a clear loud voice, as he had said in the village at that hour and season for the previous forty years –

'A merry Christmas to ye!'

When the expectant stillness consequent upon the exclamation had nearly died out of them all, an increasing light made itself visible in one of the windows of the upper floor. It came so close to the blind that the exact position of the flame could be perceived from the outside. Remaining steady for an instant, the blind went upward from before it, revealing to thirty concentrated eyes a young girl, framed as a picture by the window architrave, and unconsciously illuminating her countenance to a vivid brightness by a candle she held in her left hand, close to her face, her right hand being extended to the side of the window. She was wrapped in a white robe of some kind, whilst down her shoulders fell a twining profusion of marvellously rich hair, in a wild disorder which proclaimed it to be only during the invisible hours of the night that such a condition was discoverable. Her bright eyes were looking into the grey world outside with an uncertain expression, oscillating between courage and shyness, which, as she recognized the semicircular group of dark forms gathered before her, transformed itself into pleasant resolution.

Opening the window, she said lightly and warmly –

'Thank you, singers, thank you!'

Together went the window quickly and quietly, and the blind started downward on its return to its place. Her fair forehead and eyes vanished; her little mouth; her neck and shoulders; all of her. Then the spot of candlelight shone nebulously as before; then it moved away.

'How pretty!' exclaimed Dick Dewy.

'If she'd been rale wexwork she couldn't ha' been comelier,' said Michael Mail.

'As near a thing to a spiritual vision as ever *I* wish to see!' said tranter Dewy.

'O, sich I never, never see!' said Leaf fervently.

All the rest, after clearing their throats and adjusting their hats, agreed that such a sight was worth singing for.

'Now to Farmer Shiner's, and then replenish our insides, father?' said the tranter.

'Wi' all my heart,' said old William, shouldering his bass-viol.

24

The Christmas Goose

WILLIAM McGONAGALL

William McGonagall, self-styled 'poet and tragedian', was born in 1830, the son of a Scottish hand-loom weaver. In June 1877 he experienced what he called 'a strange kind of feeling . . . a strong desire to write poetry', and heard voices urging him to put pen to paper. Perhaps McGonagall misheard the message, or maybe the celestial voices weren't meant for him at all, since the unstoppable stream of writing which poured from him at every conceivable opportunity thereafter was anything but divine in conception or execution; it was, however, so uniquely awful that he is now assured of a place among the curiosities of English literature. His poem on the Christmas goose is a fair sample of his work, complete with atrocious rhymes and eccentric rhythms, and is interesting for McGonagall's apparent approval of the smug Smiggs' callous and selfish attitude to the plight of the 'juvenile prig' (or thief) and the poor in general.

McGonagall died in 1902, having unaccountably omitted to write his own epitaph.

> Mr Smiggs was a gentleman,
> And lived in London town;
> His wife she was a good kind soul,
> And seldom known to frown.
>
> 'Twas on Christmas eve,
> And Smiggs and his wife lay cosy in bed,
> When the thought of buying a goose
> Came into his head.
>
> So the next morning,
> Just as the sun rose,
> He jump'd out of bed,
> And he donn'd his clothes,
>
> Saying, 'Peggy, my dear,
> You need not frown,
> For I'll buy you the best goose
> In all London town.'

So away to the poultry shop he goes,
And bought the goose, as he did propose,
And for it he paid one crown,
The finest, he thought, in London town.

When Smiggs bought the goose
He suspected no harm,
But a naughty boy stole it
From under his arm.

Then Smiggs he cried, 'Stop, thief!
Come back with my goose!'
But the naughty boy laugh'd at him,
And gave him much abuse.

But a policeman captur'd the naughty boy,
And gave the goose to Smiggs,
And said he was greatly bother'd
By a set of juvenile prigs.

So the naughty boy was put in prison
For stealing the goose,
And got ten days' confinement
Before he got loose.

So Smiggs ran home to his dear Peggy,
Saying, 'Hurry, and get this fat goose ready,
That I have bought for one crown;
So, my darling, you need not frown.'

'Dear Mr Smiggs, I will not frown:
I'm sure 'tis cheap for one crown,
Especially at Christmas time –
Oh! Mr Smiggs, it's really fine.'

'Peggy, it is Christmas time,
So let us drive dull care away,
For we have got a Christmas goose,
So cook it well, I pray.

'No matter how the poor are clothed,
Or if they starve at home,
We'll drink our wine, and eat our goose,
Aye, and pick it to the bone.'

from
Lark Rise

FLORA THOMPSON

*The trilogy **Lark Rise to Candleford**, published in 1945, established Flora Thompson as a penetrating and accurate observer of the English countryside in the last decades of the nineteenth century. In her fictitious communities of Lark Rise and Candleford Green she chronicles the kind of centuries-old, traditional way of life for which other writers, like Thomas Hardy, felt such sympathy. This extract is taken from Chapter 15 of **Lark Rise**, the first book in the trilogy.*

Christmas Day passed very quietly. The men had a holiday from work and the children from school and the churchgoers attended special Christmas services. Mothers who had young children would buy them an orange each and a handful of nuts; but, except at the end house and the inn, there was no hanging up of stockings, and those who had no kind elder sister or aunt in service to send them parcels got no Christmas presents.

Still, they did manage to make a little festival of it. Every year the farmer killed an ox for the purpose and gave each of his men a joint of beef, which duly appeared on the Christmas dinner-table together with plum pudding – not Christmas pudding, but suet duff with a good sprinkling of raisins. Ivy and other evergreens (it was not a holly country) were hung from the ceiling and over the pictures; a bottle of home-made wine was uncorked, a good fire was made up, and, with doors and windows closed against the keen, wintry weather, they all settled down by their own firesides for a kind of super-Sunday. There was little visiting of neighbours and there were no family reunions, for the girls in service could not be spared at that season, and the few boys who had gone out in the world were mostly serving abroad in the Army.

There were still bands of mummers in some of the larger villages, and village choirs went carol-singing about the countryside; but none of these came to the hamlet, for they knew the collection to be expected there would not make it worth their while. A few families, sitting by their own firesides, would sing carols and songs; that, and more and better food and a better fire than usual, made up their Christmas cheer.

from
The Diary of a Nobody

GEORGE and WEEDON GROSSMITH

The Diary of a Nobody, the chronicle of a year or so in the totally undistinguished life of Charles Pooter, showing his perpetual struggle to maintain middle-class respectability in the face of the rest of the world's vulgarity, is one of the delights of late-Victorian comic literature. It was written by the Grossmith brothers, George and Weedon, and appeared originally in **Punch** magazine; it was published as a book, in a fuller version, in 1892. The diary entries for Christmas portray Pooter's high moral standards being put under severe strain, since his rectitude is shared on this festive occasion neither by his wife Carrie nor his man-about-town son Lupin.

December 24. I am a poor man, but I would gladly give ten shillings to find out who sent me the insulting Christmas card I received this morning. I never insult people; why should they insult me? The worst part of the transaction is, that I find myself suspecting all my friends. The handwriting on the envelope is evidently disguised, being written sloping the wrong way. I cannot think either Gowing or Cummings would do such a mean thing. Lupin denied all knowledge of it, and I believe him; although I disapprove of his laughing and sympathising with the offender. Mr. Franching would be above such an act; and I don't think any of the Mutlars would descend to such a course. I wonder if Pitt, that impudent clerk at the office, did it? Or Mrs. Birrell, the charwoman, or Burwin-Fosselton? The writing is too good for the former.

Christmas Day We caught the 10.20 train at Paddington, and spent a pleasant day at Carrie's mother's. The country was quite nice and pleasant, although the roads were sloppy. We dined in the middle of the day, just ten of us, and talked over old times. If everybody had a nice, *uninterfering* mother-in-law, such as I have, what a deal of happiness there would be in the world. Being all in good spirits, I proposed her health; and I made, I think, a very good speech.

I concluded, rather neatly, by saying: 'On an occasion like this – whether relatives, friends, or acquaintances, – we are all inspired with good feelings towards each other. We are of one mind, and think only of love and friendship. Those who have quarrelled with absent friends should kiss and make it up. Those who happily have *not* fallen out, can kiss all the same.'

I saw the tears in the eyes of both Carrie and her mother, and must say I felt very flattered by the compliment. That dear old Reverend John Panzy Smith, who married us, made a most cheerful and amusing speech, and said he should act on my suggestion respecting the kissing. He then walked round the table and kissed all the ladies, including Carrie. Of course one did not object to this; but I was more than staggered when a young fellow named Moss, who was a stranger to me, and who had scarcely spoken a word through dinner, jumped up suddenly with a sprig of mistletoe, and exclaimed: 'Hulloh! I don't see why I shouldn't be on in this scene.' Before one could realise what he was about to do, he kissed Carrie and the rest of the ladies.

Fortunately the matter was treated as a joke, and we all laughed; but it was a dangerous experiment, and I felt very uneasy for a moment as to the result. I subsequently referred to the matter to Carrie, but she said: 'Oh, he's not much more than a boy.' I said that he had a very large moustache for a boy. Carrie replied: 'I didn't say he was not a nice boy.'

December 26. I did not sleep very well last night; I never do in a strange bed. I feel a little indigestion, which one must expect at this time of the year. Carrie and I returned to Town in the evening. Lupin came in late. He said he enjoyed his Christmas, and added: 'I feel as fit as a Lowther Arcade fiddle, and only require a little more "oof" to feel as fit as a £500 Stradivarius.' I have long since given up trying to understand Lupin's slang, or asking him to explain it.

27

Reginald

SAKI

'Saki' (the pen-name of Hector Hugh Munro) was born in Burma in 1870, and his sister's earliest recollection of him was a nursery incident, when H.H. seized a long-handled hearth brush, plunged it into the fire, and chased her and his elder brother Charlie round the table shouting, 'I'm God! I'm going to destroy the world!' He didn't, in fact, turn out to be the author of such cosmic destruction, but his later writings, in an elegant and mischievously witty style, certainly created a few disturbing ripples among the staid and conventional society of his time; as the poet Christopher Morley said of him, 'He has the claw of the demon-cat/Beneath his brilliant robe.'

His creation 'Reginald' first appeared in the **Westminster Gazette***, and the collected stories were published in 1904. The character is, according to Saki's sister, 'a type composed of several young men, studied during his (Saki's) years of town life'. At the beginning of the First World War, Saki joined the army as a volunteer, and was killed by a German sniper near Beaumont Hamel in November 1916.*

The 'Austin' mentioned in **Reginald's Christmas Revel** *was Alfred Austin (1835–1913), who was made Poet Laureate in 1896. He wrote a good deal of verse, most of it, as the* **Oxford Companion to English Literature** *succinctly put it, 'of little merit'.*

Reginald on Christmas Presents

I wish it to be distinctly understood (said Reginald) that I don't want a 'George, Prince of Wales' Prayer-book as a Christmas present. The fact cannot be too widely known.

There ought (he continued) to be technical education classes on the science of present-giving. No one seems to have the faintest notion of what any one else wants, and the prevalent ideas on the subject are not creditable to a civilized community.

There is, for instance, the female relative in the country who 'knows a tie is always useful,' and sends you some spotted horror that you could only wear in secret or in Tottenham Court Road. It *might* have been useful had she kept it to tie up currant bushes with, when it would have served the double purpose of supporting the branches and frightening away the birds – for it is an admitted fact that the ordinary tomtit of commerce has a sounder aesthetic taste than the average female relative in the country.

Then there are aunts. They are always a difficult class to deal with in the matter of presents. The trouble is that one never catches them really young enough. By the time one has educated them to an appreciation of the fact that one does not wear red woollen mittens in the West End, they die, or quarrel with the family, or do something equally inconsiderate. That is why the supply of trained aunts is always so precarious.

There is my Aunt Agatha, *par exemple*, who sent me a pair of gloves last Christmas, and even got so far as to choose a kind that was being worn and had the correct number of buttons. But – *they were nines!* I sent them to a boy whom I hated intimately: he didn't wear them, of course, but he could have – that was where the bitterness of death came in. It was nearly as consoling as sending white flowers to his funeral. Of course I wrote and told my aunt that they were the one thing that had been wanting to make existence blossom like a rose; I am afraid she thought me frivolous – she comes from the North, where they live in the fear of Heaven and the Earl of Durham. (Reginald affects an exhaustive knowledge of things political, which furnishes an excellent excuse for not discussing them.) Aunts with a dash of foreign extraction in them are the most satisfactory in the way of understanding these things; but if you can't choose your aunt, it is wisest in the long run to choose the present and send her the bill.

Even friends of one's own set, who might be expected to know better, have curious delusions on the subject. I am *not* collecting copies of the cheaper editions of Omar Khayyam. I gave the last four that I received to the lift-boy, and I like to think of him reading them, with FitzGerald's notes, to his aged mother. Lift-boys always have aged mothers; shows such nice feeling on their part, I think.

Personally, I can't see where the difficulty in choosing suitable presents lies. No boy who had brought himself up properly could fail to appreciate one of those decorative bottles of liqueurs that are so reverently staged in Morel's window – and it wouldn't in the least matter if one did get duplicates. And there would always be the supreme moment of dreadful uncertainty whether it was *crême de menthe* or Chartreuse – like the expectant thrill on seeing your partner's hand turned up at bridge. People may say what they like about the decay of Christianity; the religious system that produced green Chartreuse can never really die.

And then, of course, there are liqueur glasses, and crystallized fruits, and tapestry curtains, and heaps of other necessaries of life that make really sensible presents – not to speak of luxuries, such as having one's bills paid, or getting something quite sweet in the way of jewellery. Unlike the alleged Good Woman of the Bible, I'm not above rubies. When found, by the way, she must have been rather a problem at Christmas-time; nothing short of a blank cheque would have fitted the situation. Perhaps it's as well that she's died out.

The great charm about me (concluded Reginald) is that I am so easily pleased. But I draw the line at a 'Prince of Wales' Prayer-book.

from
Reginald's Christmas Revel

On Christmas evening we were supposed to be specially festive in the Old English fashion. The hall was horribly draughty, but it seemed to be the proper place to revel in, and it was decorated with Japanese fans and Chinese lanterns which gave it a very Old English effect. A young lady with a confidential voice favoured us with a long recitation about a little girl who died or did something equally hackneyed, and then the Major gave us a graphic account of a struggle he had with a wounded bear. I privately wished that the bears would win sometimes on these occasions; at least they wouldn't go vapouring about it afterwards. Before we had time to recover our spirits, we were indulged with some thought-reading by a young man whom one knew instinctively had a good mother and an indifferent tailor – the sort of young man who talks unflaggingly through the thickest soup, and smooths his hair dubiously as though he thought it might hit back. The thought-reading was rather a success; he announced that the hostess was thinking about poetry, and she admitted that her mind was dwelling on one of Austin's odes. Which was near enough. I fancy she had really been wondering whether a scrag-end of mutton and some cold plum-pudding would do for the kitchen dinner next day. As a crowning dissipation, they all sat down to play progressive halma, with milk-chocolate for prizes. I've been carefully brought up, and I don't like to play games of skill for milk-chocolate, so I invented a headache and retired from the scene. I had been preceded a few minutes earlier by Miss Langshan-Smith, a rather formidable lady, who always got up at some uncomfortable hour in the morning, and gave you the impression that she had been in communication with most of the European Governments before breakfast. There was a paper pinned on her door with a signed request that she might be called particularly early on the morrow. Such an opportunity does not come twice in a lifetime. I covered up everything except the signature with another notice, to the effect that before these words should meet the eye she would have ended a misspent life, was sorry for the trouble she was giving, and would like a military funeral. A few minutes later I violently exploded an air-filled paper bag on the landing, and gave a stage moan that could have been heard in the cellars. Then I pursued my original intention and went to bed. The noise those people made in forcing open the good lady's door was positively indecorous; she resisted gallantly, but I believe they searched her for bullets for about a quarter of an hour, as if she had been a historic battlefield.

I hate travelling on Boxing Day, but one must occasionally do things that one dislikes.

Christmas Day in the Workhouse

GEORGE R. SIMS

Like several other popular Victorian poems, **Christmas Day in the Workhouse** *is known nowadays primarily for its first line and for the number of parodies it has inspired. It is something of a shock to turn to the original and find a work of considerable power. Though it pulls out all the stops and obviously lends itself to a melodramatic style of recitation, which probably helped to make it seem absurd,* **Christmas Day in the Workhouse** *remains a trenchant comment on a savage system. The author was George R. Sims (1847–1922) and the poem comes from his collection* **The Dagonet Ballads.**

1

It is Christmas Day in the Workhouse,
And the cold bare walls are bright
With garlands of green and holly,
And the place is a pleasant sight:
For with clean-washed hands and faces,
In a long and hungry line
The paupers sit at the tables,
For this is the hour they dine.

2

And the guardians and their ladies,
Although the wind is east,
Have come in their furs and wrappers,
To watch their charges feast;
To smile and be condescending,
Put pudding on pauper plates,
To be hosts at the workhouse banquet
They've paid for – with the rates.

3

Oh, the paupers are meek and lowly
With their 'Thank'ee kindly, mum's';

So long as they fill their stomachs,
What matter it whence it comes?
But one of the old men mutters,
And pushes his plate aside:
'Great God!' he cries; 'but it chokes me!
For this is the day *she* died.'

4

The guardians gazed in horror,
The master's face went white;
'Did a pauper refuse their pudding?'
'Could their ears believe aright?'
Then the ladies clutched their husbands,
Thinking the man would die,
Struck by a bolt, or something,
By the outraged One on high.

5

But the pauper sat for a moment,
Then rose 'mid a silence grim,
For the others had ceased to chatter,
And trembled in every limb.
He looked at the guardians' ladies,
Then, eyeing their lords, he said,
'I eat not the food of villains
Whose hands are foul and red:

6

'Whose victims cry for vengeance
From their dank, unhallowed graves.'
'He's drunk!' said the workhouse master.
'Or else he's mad, and raves.'
'Not drunk or mad,' cried the pauper,
'But only a hunted beast,
Who torn by the hounds and mangled,
Declines the vulture's feast.

7

'I care not a curse for the guardians,
And I won't be dragged away.
Just let me have the fit out,
It's only on Christmas Day

That black past comes to goad me,
And prey on my burning brain;
I'll tell you the rest in a whisper, –
I swear I won't shout again.

8

'Keep your hands off me, curse you!
Hear me right out to the end.
You come here to see how paupers
The season of Christmas spend.
You come here to watch us feeding,
As they watch the captured beast.
Hear why a penniless pauper
Spits on your paltry feast.

9

'Do you think I will take your bounty,
And let you smile and think
You're doing a noble action
With the parish's meat and drink?
Where is my wife, you traitors –
The poor old wife you slew?
Yes, by the God above us,
My Nance was killed by you!

10

'Last winter my wife lay dying,
Starved in a filthy den;
I had never been to the parish, –
I came to the parish then.
I swallowed my pride in coming,
For, ere the ruin came,
I held up my head as a trader,
And I bore a spotless name.

11

'I came to the parish, craving
Bread for a starving wife,
Bread for the woman who'd loved me
Through fifty years of life;
And what do you think they told me,
Mocking my awful grief?

That "the House" was open to us,
But they wouldn't give "out relief."

12

'I slunk to the filthy alley –
'Twas a cold, raw Christmas eve –
And the bakers' shops were open,
Tempting a man to thieve;
But I clenched my fists together,
Holding my head awry,
So I came to her empty-handed,
And mournfully told her why.

13

'Then I told her "the House" was open;
She had heard the ways of *that*,
For her bloodless cheeks went crimson,
And up in her rags she sat,
Crying, "Bide the Christmas here, John,
We've never had one apart;
I think I can bear the hunger, –
The other would break my heart."

14

'All through that eve I watched her,
Holding her hand in mine,
Praying the Lord, and weeping
Till my lips were salt as brine.
I asked her once if she hungered,
And as she answered "No,"
The moon shone in at the window
Set in a wreath of snow.

15

'Then the room was bathed in glory,
And I saw in my darling's eyes
The far-away look of wonder
That comes when the spirit flies;
And her lips were parched and parted,
And her reason came and went,
For she raved of her home in Devon,
Where our happiest years were spent.

16

'And the accents, long forgotten,
Came back to the tongue once more,
For she talked like the country lassie
I woo'd by the Devon shore.
Then she rose to her feet and trembled,
And fell on the rags and moaned,
And, "Give me a crust – I'm famished –
For the love of God!" she groaned.

17

'I rushed from the room like a madman,
And flew to the workhouse gate,
Crying, "Food for a dying woman!"
And the answer came, "Too late."
They drove me away with curses;
Then I fought with a dog in the street,
And tore from the mongrel's clutches
A crust he was trying to eat.

18

'Back, through the filthy by-lanes!
Back, through the trampled slush!
Up to the crazy garret,
Wrapped in an awful hush.
My heart sank down at the threshold,
And I paused with a sudden thrill,
For there in the silv'ry moonlight
My Nance lay, cold and still.

19

'Up to the blackened ceiling
The sunken eyes were cast –
I knew on those lips all bloodless
My name had been the last;
She'd called for her absent husband –
O God! had I but known! –
Had called in vain, and in anguish
Had died in that den – *alone*.

20

'Yes, there, in a land of plenty,
Lay a loving woman dead,
Cruelly starved and murdered
For a loaf of the parish bread.
At yonder gate, last Christmas,
I craved for a human life.
You, who would feast us paupers,
What of my murdered wife?

21

'There, get ye gone to your dinners;
Don't mind me in the least;
Think of the happy paupers
Eating your Christmas feast;
And when you recount their blessings
In your smug parochial way,
Say, what you did for *me*, too,
Only last Christmas Day.'

29

Christmas in India

RUDYARD KIPLING

*'The one thing that was never possible, if one had read him at all, was to forget him,' wrote George Orwell on the occasion of the death of Rudyard Kipling in 1936. And for those many people who had read him – for Kipling in his time was an enormously popular writer – his name was synonymous with India and the imperialism of the British Raj. This was hardly surprising, since Kipling was born in Bombay, and although he was sent home to England for a conventional English education, he returned to India at the age of seventeen to work as a journalist. His later writings, such as the novel **Kim**, fix permanently and memorably the impressions of the Indian continent under British rule at the turn of the century.*

*His poem 'Christmas in India', with its characteristically hypnotic rhythms, expresses the **Heimweh**, or homesickness, of an exile in an alien land.*

Dim dawn behind the tamarisks – the sky is saffron-yellow –
As the women in the village grind the corn,
And the parrots seek the river-side, each calling to his fellow
That the day, the staring Eastern Day, is born.
O the white dust on the highway! O the stenches in the byway!
O the clammy fog that hovers over earth!
And at Home they're making merry 'neath the white and scarlet
    berry –
What part have India's exiles in their mirth?

Full day behind the tamarisks – the sky is blue and staring –
As the cattle crawl afield beneath the yoke,
And they bear One o'er the field-path, who is past all hope or
    caring,
To that ghat below the curling wreaths of smoke.
Call on Rama, going slowly, as ye bear a brother lowly –
Call on Rama – he may hear, perhaps, your voice!
With our hymn-books and our psalters we appeal to other altars,
And to-day we bid 'good Christian men rejoice.'

Christmas in India

High noon behind the tamarisks – the sun is hot above us –
As at Home the Christmas Day is breaking wan.
They will drink our healths at dinner – those who tell us how they
    love us,
And forget us till another year be gone!
O the toil that knows no breaking! O the *Heimweh*, ceaseless,
    aching!
O the black dividing Sea and alien Plain!
Youth was cheap – wherefore we sold it. Gold was good – we hoped
    to hold it.
And to-day we know the fulness of our gain!

Grey dusk behind the tamarisks – the parrots fly together –
As the Sun is sinking slowly over home;
And his last ray seems to mock us shackled in a lifelong tether
That drags us back howe'er so far we roam.
Hard her service, poor her payment – she in ancient, tattered
    raiment –
India, she the grim Stepmother of our kind.
If a year of life be lent her, if her temple's shrine we enter,
The door is shut – we may not look behind.

Black night behind the tamarisks – the owls begin their chorus –
As the conches from the temple scream and bray.
With the fruitless years behind us and the hopeless years before us,
Let us honour, O my brothers, Christmas Day!
Call a truce, then, to our labours – let us feast with friends and
    neighbours,
And be merry as the custom of our caste;
For, if 'faint and forced the laughter', and if sadness follow after,
We are richer by one mocking Christmas past.

30

The Ghost of the Blue Chamber

JEROME K. JEROME

Jerome K. Jerome (1859–1927) is perhaps best known for **Three Men in a Boat**, *published in 1889, but he also wrote a considerable number of other novels, stories and poems. Christmas is the traditional time for ghost stories, and Jerome's story* **The Ghost of the Blue Chamber**, *with its ironic humour reminiscent of Saki, provides a most unconventional spook and a neat final twist.*

'I don't want to make you fellows nervous,' began my uncle in a peculiarly impressive, not to say blood-curdling, tone of voice, 'and if you would rather that I did not mention it, I won't; but, as a matter of fact, this very house, in which we are now sitting is haunted.'

'You don't say that!' exclaimed Mr. Coombes.

'What's the use of your saying I don't say it when I have just said it?' retorted my uncle somewhat annoyed. 'You talk so foolishly. I tell you the house is haunted. Regularly on Christmas Eve the Blue Chamber' (they call the room next to the nursery the 'Blue Chamber' at my uncle's) 'is haunted by the ghost of a sinful man – a man who once killed a Christmas carol singer with a lump of coal.'

'How did he do it?' asked Mr. Coombes, eagerly. 'Was it difficult?'

'I do not know how he did it,' replied my uncle; 'he did not explain the process. The singer had taken up a position just inside the front gate, and was singing a ballad. It is presumed that, when he opened his mouth for B flat, the lump of coal was thrown by the sinful man from one of the windows, and that it went down the singer's throat and choked him.'

'You want to be a good shot, but it is certainly worth trying,' murmured Mr. Coombes thoughtfully.

'But that was not his only crime, alas!' added my uncle. 'Prior to that he had killed a solo cornet player.'

'No! Is that really a fact?' exclaimed Mr. Coombes.

'Of course it's a fact,' answered my uncle testily. 'At all events, as much a fact as you can expect to get in a case of this sort.

'The poor fellow, the cornet player, had been in the neighbour-hood barely a month. Old Mr. Bishop, who kept the "Jolly Sand Boys" at the time, and from whom I had the story, said he had never known a more hard-working and energetic solo cornet player. He, the cornet player, only knew two tunes, but Mr. Bishop said that the man could not have played with more vigor, or for more hours a day, if he had known forty. The two tunes he did play were "Annie Laurie" and "Home Sweet Home"; and as regarded his perform-ance of the former melody, Mr. Bishop said that a mere child could have told what it was meant for.

'This musician – this poor, friendless artist – used to come regularly and play in this street just opposite for two hours every evening. One evening he was seen, evidently in response to an invitation, going into this very house, *but was never seen coming out of it!*'

'Did the townsfolk try offering any reward for his recovery?' asked Mr. Coombes.

'Not a penny,' replied my uncle.

'Another summer,' continued my uncle, 'a German band visited here, intending – so they announced on their arrival – to stay till the autumn.

'On the second day after their arival, the whole company, as fine and healthy a body of men as one would wish to see, were invited to dinner by this sinful man, and, after spending the whole of the next twenty-four hours in bed, left the town a broken and dyspeptic crew; the parish doctor, who had attended them giving it as his opinion that it was doubtful if they would, any of them, be fit to play an air again.'

'You – you don't know the recipe, do you?' asked Mr. Coombes.

'Unfortunately I do not,' replied my uncle; 'but the chief ingredi-ent was said to have been railway dining-room hash.

'I forget the man's other crimes,' my uncle went on; 'I used to know them all at one time, but my memory is not what it was. I do not, however, believe I am doing his memory an injustice in believing that he was not entirely unconnected with the death, and subsequent burial, of a gentleman who used to play the harp with his toes; and that neither was he altogether unresponsible for the lonely grave of an unknown stranger who had once visited the neighbourhood, an Italian peasant lad, a performer upon the barrel-organ.

'Every Christmas Eve,' said my uncle, cleaving with low impressive tones the strange awed silence that, like a shadow, seemed to have slowly stolen into and settled down upon the room, 'the ghost of this sinful man haunts the Blue Chamber, in this very house. There, from midnight until cock-crow, amid wild muffled shrieks and groans and mocking laughter and the ghostly sound of horrid blows, it does fierce phantom fight with the spirits of the solo cornet player and the murdered carol singer, assisted at intervals by the shades of the German band; while the ghost of the strangled harpist plays mad ghostly melodies with ghostly toes on the ghost of a broken harp.'

Uncle said the Blue Chamber was comparatively useless as a sleeping apartment on Christmas Eve.

'Hark!' said my uncle, raising a warning hand toward the ceiling, while we held our breath, and listened: 'Hark! I believe they are at it now – in the Blue Chamber!'

I rose up and said that *I* would sleep in the Blue Chamber.

'Never!' cried my uncle, springing up. 'You shall not put yourself in this deadly peril. Besides, the bed is not made.'

'Never mind the bed,' I replied, 'I have lived in furnished apartments for gentlemen, and have been accustomed to sleep on beds that have never been made from one year's end to the other. I am young, and have had a clear conscience now for a month. The spirits will not harm me. I may even do them some little good, and induce them to be quiet and go away. Besides, I should like to see the show.'

They tried to dissuade me from what they termed my foolhardy enterprise, but I remained firm and claimed my privilege. I was 'the guest.' 'The guest' always sleeps in the haunted chamber on Christmas Eve; it is his right.

They said that if I put it on that footing they had, of course, no answer, and they lighted a candle for me and followed me upstairs in a body.

Whether elevated by the feeling that I was doing a noble action or animated by a mere general consciousness of rectitude is not for me to say, but I went upstairs that night with remarkable buoyancy. It was as much as I could do to stop at the landing when I came to it; I felt I wanted to go on up to the roof. But, with the help of the banisters, I restrained my ambition, wished them all good-night and went in and shut the door.

Things began to go wrong with me from the very first. The candle tumbled out of the candlestick before my hand was off the lock. It kept on tumbling out again; I never saw such a slippery candle. I gave up attempting to use the candlestick at last and carried the candle about in my hand, and even then it would not keep upright. So I got wild and threw it out the window, and undressed and went to bed in the dark.

I did not go to sleep; I did not feel sleepy at all; I lay on my back looking up at the ceiling and thinking of things. I wish I could remember some of the ideas that came to me as I lay there, because they were so amusing.

I had been lying like this for half an hour or so, and had forgotten all about the ghost, when, on casually casting my eyes round the room, I noticed for the first time a singularly contented-looking phantom sitting in the easy-chair by the fire smoking the ghost of a long clay pipe.

I fancied for the moment, as most people would under similar circumstances, that I must be dreaming. I sat up and rubbed my eyes. No! It was a ghost, clear enough. I could see the back of the chair through his body. He looked over toward me, took the shadowy pipe from his lips and nodded.

The most surprising part of the whole thing to me was that I did not feel in the least alarmed. If anything I was rather pleased to see him. It was company.

I said: 'Good evening. It's been a cold day!'

He said he had not noticed it himself, but dared say I was right.

We remained silent for a few seconds, and then, wishing to put it pleasantly, I said: 'I believe I have the honour of addressing the ghost of the gentleman who had the accident with the carol singer?'

He smiled and said it was very good of me to remember it. One singer was not much to boast of, but still every little helped.

I was somewhat staggered at his answer. I had expected a groan of remorse. The ghost appeared, on the contrary, to be rather conceited over the business. I thought that as he had taken my reference to the singer so quietly perhaps he would not be offended if I questioned him about the organ grinder. I felt curious about that poor boy.

'Is it true,' I asked, 'that you had a hand in the death of that Italian peasant lad who came to the town with a barrel-organ that played nothing but Scotch airs?'

He quite fired up. 'Had a hand in it!' he exclaimed indignantly. 'Who has dared to pretend that he assisted me? I murdered the youth myself. Nobody helped me. Alone I did it. Show me the man who says I didn't.'

I calmed him. I assured him that I had never, in my own mind, doubted that he was the real and only assassin, and I went on and asked him what he had done with the body of the cornet player he had killed.

He said: 'To which one may you be alluding?'

'Oh, were there any more then?' I inquired.

He smiled and gave a little cough. He said he did not like to appear to be boasting, but that, counting trombones, there were seven.

'Dear me!' I replied, 'you must have had quite a busy time of it, one way and another.'

He said that perhaps he ought not to be the one to say so; but that really, speaking of ordinary middle-class society, he thought there were few ghosts who could look back upon a life of more sustained usefulness.

He puffed away in silence for a few seconds while I sat watching him. I had never seen a ghost smoking a pipe before, that I could remember, and it interested me.

I asked him what tobacco he used, and he replied: 'The ghost of cut cavendish as a rule.'

He explained that the ghost of all the tobacco that a man smoked in life belonged to him when he became dead. He said he himself had smoked a good deal of cut cavendish when he was alive, so that he was well supplied with the ghost of it now.

I thought I would join him in a pipe, and he said, 'Do, old man'; and I reached over and got out the necessary paraphernalia from my coat pocket and lit up.

We grew quite chummy after that, and he told me all his crimes. He said he had lived next door once to a young lady who was learning to play the guitar, while a gentleman who practiced on the bass-viol lived opposite. And he, with fiendish cunning, had introduced these two unsuspecting young people to one another, and had persuaded them to elope with each other against their parents' wishes, and take their musical instruments with them; and they

94

had done so, and before the honeymoon was over, *she* had broken his head with the bass-viol, and he had tried to cram the guitar down her throat, and had injured her for life.

My friend said he used to lure muffin-men into the passage and then stuff them with their own wares till they burst. He said he had quieted eighteen that way.

Young men and women who recited long and dreary poems at evening parties, and callow youths who walked about the streets late at night, playing concertinas, he used to get together and poison in batches of ten, so as to save expenses; and park orators and temperance lecturers he used to shut up six in a small room with a glass of water and a collection-box apiece, and let them talk each other to death.

It did one good to listen to him.

I asked him when he expected the other ghosts – the ghosts of the singer and the cornet player, and the German band that Uncle John had mentioned. He smiled, and said they would never come again, any of them.

I said, 'Why, isn't it true, then, that they meet you here every Christmas Eve for a row?'

He replied that it was true. Every Christmas Eve, for twenty-five years, had he and they fought in that room; but they would never trouble him or anybody else again. One by one had he laid them out, spoiled and made them utterly useless for all haunting purposes. He had finished off the last German band ghost that very evening, just before I came upstairs, and had thrown what was left of it out through the slit between the window sashes. He said it would never be worth calling a ghost again.

'I suppose you will still come yourself, as usual?' I said. 'They would be sorry to miss you, I know.'

'Oh, I don't know,' he replied; 'there's nothing much to come for now; unless,' he added kindly, '*you* are going to be here. I'll come if you will sleep here next Christmas Eve.'

'I have taken a liking to you,' he continued; 'you don't fly off, screeching, when you see a party, and your hair doesn't stand on end. You've no idea,' he said, 'how sick I am of seeing people's hair standing on end.'

He said it irritated him.

Just then a slight noise reached us from the yard below, and he started and turned deathly black.

'You are ill,' I cried, springing toward him; 'tell me the best thing to do for you. Shall I drink some brandy, and give you the ghost of it?'

He remained silent, listening intently for a moment, and then he gave a sigh of relief, and the shade came back to his cheek.

'It's all right,' he murmured; 'I was afraid it was the cock.'

'Oh, it's too early for that,' I said. 'Why, it's only the middle of the night.'

'Oh, that doesn't make any difference to those cursed chickens,' he replied bitterly. 'They would just as soon crow in the middle of the night as at any other time – sooner, if they thought it would spoil a chap's evening out. I believe they do it on purpose.'

He said a friend of his, the ghost of a man who had killed a tax collector, used to haunt a house in Long Acre, where they kept fowls in the cellar, and every time a policeman went by and flashed his searchlight down the grating, the old cock there would fancy it was the sun, and start crowing like mad, when, of course, the poor ghost had to dissolve, and it would, in consequence, get back home sometimes as early as one o'clock in the morning, furious because it had only been out for an hour.

I agreed that it seemed very unfair.

'Oh, it's an absurd arrangement altogether,' he continued, quite angrily. 'I can't imagine what our chief could have been thinking of when he made it. As I have said to him, over and over again, "Have a fixed time, and let everybody stick to it – say four o'clock in summer, and six in winter. Then one would know what one was about."'

'How do you manage when there isn't any clock handy?' I inquired.

He was on the point of replying, when again he started and listened. This time I distinctly heard Mr. Bowles' cock, next door, crow twice.

'There you are,' he said, rising and reaching for his hat; 'that's the sort of thing we have to put up with. What *is* the time?'

I looked at my watch, and found it was half-past three.

'I thought as much,' he muttered. 'I'll wring that blessed bird's neck if I get hold of it.' And he prepared to go.

'If you can wait half a minute,' I said, getting out of bed, 'I'll go a bit of the way with you.'

'It's very good of you,' he replied, pausing, 'but it seems unkind to drag you out.'

'Not at all,' I replied; 'I shall like a walk.' And I partially dressed myself, and took my umbrella; and he put his arm through mine, and we went out together, the best of friends.

from
From Mons to Ypres with French

FREDERIC COLEMAN

Most people have heard of the occasion during the first Christmas of the 1914–18 War, when, along certain sections of trenches, the Christmas spirit of international goodwill overcame for a short time the spirit of nationalism and enmity. The following description of the incident comes from a book published in 1916, by Frederic Coleman, an American reporter who spent the first year of the war with the British Expeditionary Force in France and Flanders. Coleman was not present at the occasion, but it was described to him a few days later by men who were, so the account has the freshness of immediate experience.

Christmastide found the British Army becoming accustomed to the stagnation of a winter campaign in sodden Flanders. On Christmas Eve, at midnight, the Germans in the trenches in front of Ploegsteert Wood began to sing Christmas songs in chorus. The Somersets faced them, and a couple of Somerset bandsmen, who had left their instruments in England and were assigned to stretcher-bearing, told me a day or so after Christmas what occurred at Ploegsteert on Christmas Day.

The German Christmas songs of the night before had odd results.

'The songs was fine,' one of my informants declared. 'They sang a lot. But the best was to come. A German bloke had a cornet, and he could play it grand. He just made it talk. The songs and the tunes the cornet feller played seemed more and more like ones we knew. At last out came that cornet with "Home, Sweet Home", and nobody could keep still. We all sang – Huns, English and all.'

The night spent in song produced a general peacefulness of spirit all round. As day broke the Somersets saw the Saxons on top of their trenches. Soon they called out, 'Come over and visit us, we are Saxons.' No shots were fired.

'None of our chaps started for the German trenches,' continued the bandsman. 'We had heard all about the white flags the Bosches had fired from under and all that. But our medical officer is a funny cove, and he got an idea in his head that started the whole thing. He said he saw a chance to give a burial to some of our dead that had been lying between trenches no end of a while. So he told me and my pal here to follow him, and afore we knew where he was going, up he pops on the trench parapet. The Bosch trenches was only fifty to seventy yards in front, and up we had to get, and over after that doctor.

'One of the Saxon fellers who spoke pretty good English sung out and said we could go right on with what we were doing. He said all of us could bury dead till four o'clock, and they would, too. And sure enough they did get at it pretty soon afterward. Some of our chaps changed cigars and cigarettes with them Huns, and had talks about all sorts of things. At four o'clock we all took cover on both sides, but there was no firing on our front that night. The next morning we kept up the calling out business. We didn't stop it for a matter of eight days.'

from
Cider with Rosie

LAURIE LEE

Growing up in a remote Cotswold village in the years immediately following the First World War, Laurie Lee was just in time to experience a way of life that was soon to vanish before the tide of encroaching urbanism and sophisticated technology which we now take as the hallmark of our own day. The following account of village carol-singing, taken from **Cider with Rose**, *can be compared with Thomas Hardy's earlier description, evoking as it does a rural society in which social gradations are still clearly defined, and the Squire, old and vague as he is, is still accorded due deference.*

The week before Christmas, when snow seemed to lie thickest, was the moment for carol-singing; and when I think back to those nights it is to the crunch of snow and to the lights of the lanterns on it. Carol-singing in my village was a special tithe for the boys, the girls had little to do with it. Like hay-making, blackberrying, stone-clearing, and wishing-people-a-happy-Easter, it was one of our seasonal perks.

By instinct we knew just when to begin it; a day too soon and we should have been unwelcome, a day too late and we should have received lean looks from people whose bounty was already exhausted. When the true moment came, exactly balanced, we recognized it and were ready.

So as soon as the wood had been stacked in the oven to dry for the morning fire, we put on our scarves and went out through the streets, calling loudly between our hands, till the various boys who knew the signal ran out from their houses to join us.

One by one they came stumbling over the snow, swinging their lanterns around their heads, shouting and coughing horribly.

'Coming carol-barking then?'

We were the Church Choir, so no answer was necessary. For a year we had praised the Lord out of key, and as a reward for this service – on top of the Outing – we now had the right to visit all the big houses, to sing our carols and collect our tribute.

To work them all in meant a five-mile foot journey over wild and generally snowed-up country. So the first thing we did was to plan our route; a formality, as the route never changed. All the same, we blew on our fingers and argued; and then we chose our Leader. This was not binding, for we all fancied ourselves as Leaders, and he who started the night in that position usually trailed home with a bloody nose.

Eight of us set out that night. There was Sixpence the Tanner, who had never sung in his life (he just worked his mouth in church); the brothers Horace and Boney, who were always fighting everybody and always getting the worst of it; Clergy Green, the preaching maniac; Walt the bully, and my two brothers. As we went down the lane other boys, from other villages, were already about the hills, bawling 'Kingwenslush', and shouting through keyholes 'Knock on the knocker! Ring at the Bell! Give us a penny for singing so well!' They weren't an approved charity as we were, the Choir; but competition was in the air.

Our first call as usual was the house of the Squire, and we trouped nervously down his drive. For light we had candles in marmalade-jars suspended on loops of string, and they threw pale gleams on the towering snowdrifts that stood on each side of the drive. A blizzard was blowing, but we were well wrapped up, with Army puttees on our legs, woollen hats on our heads, and several scarves around our ears.

As we approached the Big House across its white silent lawns, we too grew respectfully silent. The lake near by was stiff and black, the waterfall frozen and still. We arranged ourselves shuffling around the big front door, then knocked and announced the Choir.

A maid bore the tidings of our arrival away into the echoing distances of the house, and while we waited we cleared our throats noisily. Then she came back, and the door was left ajar for us, and we were bidden to begin. We brought no music, the carols were in our heads. 'Let's give 'em "Wild Shepherds",' said Jack. We began in confusion, plunging into a wreckage of keys, of different words and tempo; but we gathered our strength; he who sang loudest took the rest of us with him, and the carol took shape if not sweetness.

This huge stone house, with its ivied walls, was always a mystery to us. What were those gables, those rooms and attics, those narrow windows veiled by the cedar trees? As we sang 'Wild Shepherds' we craned our necks, gaping into that lamplit hall which we had never entered; staring at the muskets and untenanted chairs, the great tapestries furred by dust – until suddenly, on the stairs, we saw the old Squire himself standing and listening with his head on one side.

He didn't move until we'd finished; then slowly he tottered towards us, dropped two coins in our box with a trembling hand, scratched his name in the book we carried, gave us each a long look with his moist blind eyes, then turned away in silence.

As though released from a spell, we took a few sedate steps, then broke into a run for the gate. We didn't stop till we were out of the grounds. Impatient, at last, to discover the extent of his bounty, we squatted by the cowsheds, held our lanterns over the book, and saw that he had written 'Two Shillings'. This was quite a good start. No one of any worth in the district would dare to give us less than the Squire.

So with money in the box, we pushed on up the valley, pouring scorn on each other's performance. Confident now, we began to consider our quality and whether one carol was not better suited to us than another. Horace, Walt said, shouldn't sing at all; his voice was beginning to break. Horace disputed this and there was a brief token battle – they fought as they walked, kicking up divots of snow, then they forgot it, and Horace still sang.

Steadily we worked through the length of the valley, going from house to house, visiting the lesser and the greater gentry – the farmers, the doctors, the merchants, the majors, and other exalted persons. It was freezing hard and blowing too; yet not for a moment did we feel the cold. The snow blew into our faces, into our eyes and mouths, soaked through our puttees, got into our boots, and dripped from our woollen caps. But we did not care. The collecting-box grew heavier, and the list of names in the book longer and more extravagant, each trying to outdo the other.

Mile after mile we went, fighting against the wind, falling into snowdrifts, and navigating by the lights of the houses. And yet we never saw our audience. We called at house after house; we sang in courtyards and porches, outside windows, or in the damp gloom of hallways; we heard voices from hidden rooms; we smelt rich clothes and strange hot food; we saw maids bearing in dishes or carrying away coffee-cups; we received nuts, cakes, figs, preserved ginger, dates, cough-drops, and money; but we never once saw our patrons. We sang as it were at the castle walls, and apart from the Squire, who had shown himself to prove that he was still alive, we never expected it otherwise.

As the night drew on there was trouble with Boney. 'Noël', for instance, had a rousing harmony which Boney persisted in singing, and singing flat. The others forbade him to sing it at all, and Boney said he would fight us. Picking himself up, he agreed we were right, then he disappeared altogether. He just turned away and walked into the snow and wouldn't answer when we called him back. Much later, as we reached a far point up the valley, somebody said 'Hark!' and we stopped to listen. Far away across the fields from the distant village came the sound of a frail voice singing, singing 'Noël', and singing it flat – it was Boney, branching out on his own.

We approached our last house high up on the hill, the place of Joseph the farmer. For him we had chosen a special carol, which was about the other Joseph, so that we always felt that singing it added a spicy cheek to the night. The last stretch of country to reach his farm was perhaps the most difficult of all. In these rough bare lanes, open to all winds, sheep were buried and wagons lost. Huddled together, we tramped in one another's footsteps, powdered snow blew into our screwed-up eyes, the candles burnt low, some blew out altogether, and we talked loudly above the gale.

Crossing, at last, the frozen mill-stream – whose wheel in summer still turned a barren mechanism – we climbed up to Joseph's farm. Sheltered by trees, warm on its bed of snow, it seemed always to be like this. As always it was late; as always this was our final call. The snow had a fine crust upon it, and the old trees sparkled like tinsel.

We grouped ourselves round the farmhouse porch. The sky cleared, and broad streams of stars ran down over the valley and away to Wales. On Slad's white slopes, seen through the black sticks of its woods, some red lamps still burned in the windows.

Everything was quiet; everywhere there was the faint crackling silence of the winter night. We started singing, and we were all moved by the words and the sudden trueness of our voices. Pure, very clear, and breathless we sang:

As Joseph was a walking
He heard an angel sing;
'This night shall be the birth-time
Of Christ the Heavenly King.

He neither shall be bornèd
In Housen nor in hall,
Nor in a place of paradise
But in an ox's stall . . .'

And two thousand Christmases became real to us then; the houses, the halls, the places of paradise had all been visited; the stars were bright to guide the Kings through the snow; and across the farmyard we could hear the beasts in their stalls. We were given roast apples and hot mince-pieces, in our nostrils were spices like myrrh, and in our wooden box, as we headed back for the village, there were golden gifts for all.

33

William's Truthful Christmas

RICHMAL CROMPTON

William Brown, Richmal Crompton's unwitting anarchist, made his first appearance as an eleven-year-old in 1922, and remained at that age until the last volume of his adventures was published in 1966, during which time he had featured in thirty-seven books, totalling some 350 separate stories.

Originally written for adults, the William stories found immense favour among younger readers, and the best of them contain some of the most amusing writing, the funniest social comment and the neatest plotting ever to appear in children's fiction. William's views on Christmas were never very enthusiastic: as far as he was concerned, it was a rather dreary interruption to the rich complications of his everyday life, and brought with it the necessity for good behaviour, a plague of usually nauseating relations, and 'useful' unexciting presents (William would have warmed to Saki's Reginald). The following passage is from the story 'William's Truthful Christmas', from the fifth volume of William stories, **Still William**, *published in 1925, and describes what happens when William decides to take literally the earnest injunction of the vicar to 'speak the truth one with another and cast aside deceit and hypocrisy' during the Christmas season.*

William awoke early on Christmas day. He had hung up his stocking the night before and was pleased to see it fairly full. He took out the presents quickly but not very optimistically. He had been early disillusioned in the matter of grown-ups' capacity for choosing suitable presents. Memories of prayer books and history books and socks and handkerchiefs floated before his mental vision . . . Yes, as bad as ever! . . . a case containing a pen and pencil and ruler, a new brush and comb, a purse (empty) and a new tie . . . a penknife and a box of toffee were the only redeeming features. On the chair by his bedside was a book of Church History from Aunt Emma and a box containing a pair of compasses, a protractor and a set square from Uncle Frederick . . .

William dressed, but as it was too early to go down he sat on the floor and ate all his tin of toffee. Then he turned his attention to his

Church History book. He read a few pages but the character and deeds of the saintly Aidan so exasperated him that he was driven to relieve his feeling by taking his new pencil from its case and adorning the saint's picture by the addition of a top hat and spectacles. He completed the alterations by a moustache and by changing the book the saint held into an attaché case. He made similar alterations to every picture in the book . . . St. Oswald seemed much improved by them and this cheered William considerably. Then he took his penknife and began to carve his initials upon his brush and comb . . .

William appeared at breakfast wearing his new tie and having brushed his hair with his new brush or rather with what was left of his new brush after his very drastic initial carving. He carried under his arm his presents for his host and hostess. He exchanged 'Happy Christmas' gloomily. His resolve to cast away deceit and hypocrisy and speak the truth one with another lay heavy upon him. He regarded it as an obligation that could not be shirked. William was a boy of great tenacity of purpose. Having once made up his mind to a course he pursued it regardless of consequences . . .

'Well, William, darling,' said his mother. 'Did you find your presents?'

'Yes,' said William gloomily. 'Thank you.'

'Did you like the book and instruments that Uncle and I gave you?' said Aunt Emma brightly.

'No,' said William gloomily and truthfully. 'I'm not int'rested in Church History an' I've got something like those at school. Not that I'd want 'em,' he added hastily, 'if I hadn't 'em.'

'*William!*' screamed Mrs. Brown in horror. 'How can you be so ungrateful!'

'I'm not ungrateful,' explained William wearily. 'I'm only bein' truthful. I'm casting aside deceit an' . . . an' hyp-hyp-what he said. I'm only sayin' that I'm not int'rested in Church History nor in those inst'ments. But thank you very much for 'em.'

There was a gasp of dismay and a horrified silence during which William drew his paper packages from under his arm.

'Here are your Christmas presents from me,' he said.

The atmosphere brightened. They unfastened their parcels with expressions of anticipation and Christian forgiveness upon their faces.

William watched them, his face 'registering' only patient suffering.

'It's very kind of you,' said Aunt Emma, still struggling with the string.

'It's not kind,' said William, still treading doggedly the path of truth. 'Mother said I'd got to bring you something.'

Mrs. Brown coughed suddenly and loudly but not in time to drown the fatal words of truth . . .

'But still—er—very kind,' said Aunt Emma though with less enthusiasm.

At last she brought out a small pincushion.

'Thank you very much, William,' she said. 'You really oughtn't to have spent your money on me like this.'

'I din't,' said William stonily. 'I hadn't any money, but I'm very glad you like it. It was left over from Mother's stall at the Sale of Work, an' Mother said it was no use keepin' it for nex' year because it had got so faded.'

Again Mrs. Brown coughed loudly but too late. Aunt Emma said coldly:

'I see. Yes. Your mother was quite right. But thank you all the same, William.'

Uncle Frederick had now taken the wrappings from his present and held up a leather purse.

'Ah, this is a really useful present,' he said jovially.

'I'm 'fraid it's not very useful,' said William. 'Uncle Jim sent it to father for his birthday but father said it was no use 'cause the catch wouldn' catch so he gave it to me to give to you.'

Uncle Frederick tried the catch.

'Um . . . ah . . .' he said. 'Your father was quite right. The catch won't catch. Never mind, I'll send it back to your father as a New Year present . . . what?'

As soon as the Brown family were left alone it turned upon William in a combined attack.

'I *warned* you!' said Ethel to her mother.

'He ought to be hung,' said Robert.

'William, how *could* you?' said Mrs. Brown.

'When I'm bad, you go on at me,' said William with exasperation, 'an' when I'm tryin' to lead a holier life and cast aside hyp–hyp– what he said, you go on at me. I dunno what I *can* be. I don't mind bein' hung. I'd as soon be hung as keep havin' Christmas over an' over again simply every year the way we do . . .'

34

Christmas with the Cheggies

DOLLY SCANNELL

*Brought up in the East End of London in a family of ten children, Dolly Scannell experienced poverty and hardship in her early life, but nevertheless she lived in an atmosphere of love, optimism and eternal good humour. In her first book, **Mother Knew Best** (the only thing she had written since winning a school essay competition at the age of twelve), she captures the close family spirit of the London East End, which found its strongest expression at Christmas-time.*

There is something very satisfying about being a big frog in a small pond, and my twelfth year was one of my happiest. I convinced myself it was fortunate I had failed the scholarship, for life would have been learning and homework. I would have been one of the masses, whereas now I need do no schoolwork, but just lord it around the school with my little P badge; why, I was as good as a mistress. And in this year, 1923, I had the Christmas of my life, enough joy, I felt, to last me for ever.

Christmas was always a magic time for us, there was a smell in the air quite different from any other season. I had grown out of putting my sock at the end of the bed. After all, what was the point, the fruit we used to find in our socks would be in bowls in the front room now. This special Christmas I had stocked up with books from the library and Mother was busy on Christmas Eve with the usual mince-pie-making and goose-stuffing. I was glad we had a goose again. The last Christmas we had sat down to an enormous baked rabbit, when it dawned on us all that it was the rabbit from the hutch in the back yard. Father had murdered it and none of us would eat it. I couldn't possibly eat a pet, a friend, and Father had grumbled and sworn that we should all know what it was like to be starving. Mother said he lost his temper because he had a guilty conscience. We never kept a pet rabbit again.

Agnes and Arthur were married, Charlie was a sailor, Winifred was at the bank, Leonard a sailor, Amy in a local office, David at Sir

John Cass School, Cecil in an office in Bow, Marjorie and I were at school. This Christmas we would all be together.

The family were all up when lazy Marjorie and I came down to a surprise which made us both speechless. We had never had presents at Christmas and our two places at the table were piled high. Shiny pencil-boxes with flowers on them, pens, pencils, books, red woollen gloves, sweets, a new frock. The whole family gazed and laughed at our faces, and Mother wiped her eyes. She always seemed to me to shed a few tears at the wrong things. I had such a lot of books: *What Katy Did*, *What Katy Did Next*, *What Katy Did at School*. I think Marjorie burst into tears as well.

We spent the afternoon after Christmas dinner going over our presents. I kept wrapping mine up, putting them away in a safe place, then getting them all out again. 'Now, Dolly,' said Mother, 'use them, enjoy them, don't put them away and never have the wear out of them.'

Father was always affable at Christmastime; I loved the smell of his cigar and the way he winked at Mother and me. Meals were never late in our house. My friends had to wait until their fathers came home from the public houses, but my father never went to a public house, he went to his club where they played snooker, skittles, darts, etc., and he always came home for dinner at one o'clock. Tea was at 4.30 and supper at 7.30. I suppose this sticking to routine made my friends sure we were different. But it was lovely for us, especially at Christmastime; we seemed to have hours and hours more time for festivities than my friends, for theirs was a 'hanging-about' time waiting for their fathers. When their mothers were washing up after dinner we had even had Christmas tea and were beginning our fun.

After tea we turned on the gramophone. It was a square mahogany box with a large green horn, and we had records of 'The Laughing Policeman', Nellie Wallace, George Robey and Dame Clara Butt. As the sailor boys came home from sea more were added to our collection.

It was after tea that the fun started, for my eldest brothers and sisters had invited friends home. We played the writing games first, Consequences, and of course, my favourite, Towns, Countries, Rivers. There was always much argument as to which letter we would use each time, and usually Winnie settled this by taking the first letter on the page from a book she would open at random.

Great cries if she hit on the same letter twice in a row. The game went on for some time, usually ending when the arguments got too fierce and the answers could not be checked in the huge dictionary Winnie had won at George Green's School.

Having got the guests appreciably settled, Father would disappear downstairs to his barrel and his Zane Grey or Jack London book, and now the celebrations really began. The whole family, except myself, did a turn. Agnes told a sad story, Arthur sang 'The Cornish Floral Dance' in a sort of quavering baritone (I felt shy and wouldn't look at him). Charlie played the mandoline, Amy frightened us all with the 'Green Eye of the Little Yellow God,' and at the applause, which was exceptional and meant, to Amy, an encore, she began 'Lascar' by Alfred Noyes. But whoever was master of ceremonies cut this encore short as there were many more performers yet. Not like me, Amy thought. I think she was right, and I was always jealous of her dramatic bent and lovely voice. David told a few jokes at which the boys screamed and Mother tutted. Cecil sang a song, for he had been in the church choir.

I did nothing and no one pressed me about this. By tacit consent there was really nothing Dolly could do, and little Marjorie, who had left the room, now returned dressed in a sort of pale green rag. She was to do her nymph's dance, of which she was the sole proud performer and choreographer. Mother always gazed very fondly and proudly at Marjorie as she cavorted round the room in bare feet, gazing into the woods and ferns of nymphland, and we all clapped Marjorie very loudly. I admired her for her bravery and was also jealous of her achievement. She was very pretty and always chosen for the princess or heroine in the school plays when I was the old wicked king, or Scrooge. Amy said I should take that as a compliment, but I would much rather have been the beautiful heroine.

None of the guests performed. 'We would rather enjoy watching,' they all said politely. Then we had games. Snap-apple: with such a crowd of people the apples had constantly to be restrung, but mother had set aside the round ones with strong stalks before Christmas. Snap-apple was taken in turns by seniority so I came after Cecil, which was not nice in one way for, always so vicious to the apple and determined to split it, he usually split his lip instead, so the apple had little flecks of Cecil's blood on it when it came to my turn, but of course through Cecil's vigour I achieved a bit, then

I received my applause of the evening.

We played Family Coach, where Arthur told such a wonderful tale that most of us were caught, so engrossed were we with his story. We put the Tail on the Donkey, Mother loved that game. We played All Birds Fly, and laughed when one of the guests raised his hand at 'elephants fly.' It took ages for everybody to do their forfeits. And there were the super games where you can catch people who haven't played the game, and so it was lovely to have guests, for sometimes they knew games we didn't and vice versa.

This Christmas we played Confessions. Arthur dressed up as a clergyman and in his flat country vicar's hat he balanced a large amount of water. As each person entered the room he had to kneel in front of the priest and confess his sins, and when the priest bent to give him absolution so of course he would be soaked with water. Mother insisted each sinner wear a thick towel round his shoulders, for this game worried her. Arthur told the absolution-seekers the towel was the confessional surplice. Cecil's friend brought the house down because, not knowing the game, he confessed he had been extra sinful and had stolen Aldgate Pump.

We played silent charades, acting charades; Amy and I got together on charades, for it was our favourite game of the evening. I had the good ideas and she could act so perfectly.

In one way Christmas was marred for Winnie, but she never let it rankle. She had wanted a pair of brown boots all her life. Mother had said, when Winifred was little, and pleaded for these brown boots, 'When you grow up and go out to work you will be able to buy a pair of brown boots, but you will never be able to buy another stomach.' Mother couldn't manage two pairs of boots for Winnie and she had to wear black for school. Well, Winifred had now bought these brown boots, the best quality obtainable, but she had got them soaking wet in the rain, and Mother suggested she place them in the oven by the side of the kitchen fire at night when she went to bed; the warmth remaining in the oven after the fire was out would gently dry the boots.

Alas, many fires were lit before Winnie remembered the boots. Mother drew them from the oven with a cloth because they were so hot. We all looked at Winnie, for the boots were perfect pantomime boots and could have done service for a male comic or an Arabian magician. Mother started to laugh, she tried not to, but the boots were so comical and Winnie's face so unusually tragic and out of character, that what with the glass of port wine Father had given us all, even Marjorie and me (well, ours were little glasses), and the boys laughing, Winnie began to whoop with the rest of us. We were calm again until Mother said, 'It was so strange. All the week I kept smelling something and couldn't trace it,' and off we all went again.

The oven beside the fire caught Mother out many times, for in a hot summer she would put the butter in the oven, it was cool there, and Father often lit a fire on a summer evening, he always felt the cold. The butter was never thought about until it ran out all oily. Mother was often caught out with her puddings too. Christmas puddings needed hours and hours of boiling and Mother made so many she often went to bed tired and left the puddings boiling with a note to the last one in either to change the puddings over, or to turn the gas out, for we had a gas stove now. Each older member of the family carried out Mother's instructions and the puddings all had to be boiled again for mother never knew which ones had been changed or not. Father thought women stupid and disorganised, but Mother never knew which member of the family would arrive home last, and so she couldn't put the name on the note. It was arranged in the end that the one who changed the puddings over should write on the note. No one made puddings like mother and she would not put the mixture in the basins until every member of the family had stirred the stiff mixture and wished. These wishes we all took seriously and knew they would come true, but we little ones had a job to stir the stiff rich-smelling mixture and Mother had to help us.

We never minded going to bed on Christmas night, for one thing we were tired, and for another we had Boxing Day to look forward to. In our house it was Christmas Day all over again.

from
The Diary of a Provincial Lady

E.M. DELAFIELD

*The Diary of a Provincial Lady, published in 1930, is in the tradition of **The Diary
of a Nobody**. It details one year in the life of a fictitious lady of the upper middle
class who, through her daily comments, gently satirizes the manners, customs and
attitudes of her section of society.*

December 24th. – Take entire family to children's party at neighbouring Rectory. Robin says Damn three times in the Rector's
hearing, an expression never used by him before or since, but
apparently reserved for this unsuitable occasion. Party otherwise
highly successful, except that I again meet recent arrival at the
Grange, on whom I have not yet called. She is a Mrs. Somers, and is
said to keep Bees. Find myself next to her at tea, but cannot think of
anything to say about Bees, except Does she *like* them, which
sounds like a bad riddle, so leave it unsaid and talk about Preparatory Schools instead. (Am interested to note that no two parents
ever seem to have heard of one another's Preparatory Schools.
Query: Can this indicate an undue number of these establishments
throughout the country?)

   After dinner, get presents ready for children's stockings. William
unfortunately steps on small glass article of doll's furniture intended
for Vicky, but handsomely offers a shilling in compensation, which
I refuse. Much time taken up in discussing this. At eleven p.m.
children still wide awake. Angela suggests Bridge and asks Who is
that Mrs. Somers we met at the Rectory, who seems to be interested
in Bees? (A. evidently more skilled than myself in social amenities,
but do not make this comment aloud.)

Xmas Day. – Festive, but exhausting, Christmas. Robin and Vicky
delighted with everything, and spend much of the day eating.
Vicky presents her Aunt Angela with small square of canvas on
which blue donkey is worked in cross-stitch. Do not know whether

to apologise for this or not, but eventually decide better to say nothing, and hint to Mademoiselle that other design might have been preferable.

The children perhaps rather too much *en évidence*, as Angela, towards tea-time, begins to tell me that the little Maitlands have such a delightful nursery, and always spend entire day in it except when out for long walks with governess and dogs.

William asks if that Mrs. Somers is one of the Dorsetshire lot – a woman who knows about Bees. Make a note that I really must call on Mrs. S. early next week. Read up something about Bees before going.

Turkey and plum-pudding cold in the evening, to give the servants a rest. Angela looks at bulbs, and says What made me think they would be in flower for Christmas? Do not reply to this, but suggest early bed for us all.

from
Yorkshire Relish

ELIZABETH CRAGOE

*The title of Elizabeth Cragoe's autobiography, **Yorkshire Relish**, is an apt one, since the book manages to convey that individual and tangy flavour of life particular to northern England. The author was the daughter of a doctor in Knearsley, Yorkshire, and the Christmases remembered in this extract are those of the 1930s, just before the Second World War.*

Christmas Day itself began early. When we were little we would find our presents in bulging pillow-cases at the end of our beds, but by the end of the war we were too old for this, and the present-giving ceremony took place after breakfast.

Breakfast itself was entirely traditional. The ham that had hung on its hook in the cellar was boiled whole in the big, black, salmon-sized fish-kettle, then stripped of its skin and coated with golden raspings, and it was ham that formed the basis of our breakfast year by year. It was so easy. The ham, with one of Papa's deadly knives, was put on the serving table in the dining room with a loaf or two, the toaster, the Cona coffee machine and an enormous pot of stinging-fresh mustard, and everybody carved for themselves as they came down. It was immensely convenient as well as a great treat in itself and for my part I ask for no better a breakfast at any time of the year than a pink, fresh, mellow, moist home-boiled ham.

After breakfast had been eaten and cleared away, we all went into the drawing room where the presents were distributed and un-wrapped, to the accompaniment of a lot of promiscuous thank-you kissing – powdery, scented kissings of aunts aimed over your shoulder for the mutual protection of lipstick, rib-cracking, hearty, fresh-shaved-cheek kisses of uncles, dimples and blushes from cousins – it was all a great whirl as one navigated on one's voyage of thankfulness through the ever-rising tide of paper among the drawing-room chairs.

A glance at the clock brought the thanking and present-showing to an end and everybody bustled upstairs with their new-found possessions while the paper was hastily swept away. For we always had a few people in to drinks on Christmas morning, and at least a semblance of decency must be restored to the room before the visitors should arrive. The vicar and his wife always came, hot from Matins, and the partners and their wives, and occasionally a patient or two, and scarcely were they all absorbed, glass in hand, into the milling throng that was our family than the moment would be upon us that more than anything else epitomised Christmas for me – the arrival of the Salvation Army.

Year after year they streamed modestly into our garden by the little green door in the high wall that was hardly ever used, ranged themselves into a big semi-circle on the sodden top lawn between the wych elm and the weeping ash, coughed, shook the spit from their instruments, and began to play in the raw, grey, misty air. It was always the same tune, 'Hail, Smiling Morn'. Somehow you never seem to hear this piece anywhere outside Yorkshire, yet in that county it is the number one choice for Christmas music, giving points and a beating to even 'Hark the Herald' and 'O come, all ye faithful'.

So every year they stood in a half-moon and played it for us while we opened the front door and went out onto the steps and we all beamed at one another; and then one of the sisters would come up with a collecting tin and Thomas and the Uncles would all stuff folded-up pound notes into it, and they would ask us for requests and play two or three more carols for us, 'Christians Awake,' perhaps, or 'While Shepherds Watched,' or 'See Amid the Winter Snow.' Then they would shake out their instruments again and troop away with many cries of 'Merry Christmas', into the long, bare-treed street.

from
About My Father's Business

LILIAN BECKWITH

Lilian Beckwith made her reputation as a writer with her series of books about life in the Scottish islands of the Hebrides. In her autobiographical account of her early days as the daughter of a Cheshire shopkeeper, **About my Father's Business,** *she describes the family Christmases she remembers during the inter-war years.*

Her unusual nickname, Chipcart, was an invention of her father, but its derivation is not explained in the book.

Although Christmas celebrations were confined to the two weeks of the festival, preparations behind the scenes in the shop began several weeks earlier. Father bought in extra dried fruit in good time for people to bake their cakes, and despite all the extra sieving and cleaning it meant for me my task was made less tedious by knowing I was doing something connected with all the fun and glamour of Christmas. Mother made mincemeat in a huge earthenware crock, where it was left to mature for a month before it was ready for sale to customers, who brought their own jars. It was wonderful mincemeat and I used to have permanent diarrhoea during that month because I could never pass the crock without stealing a spoonful. It was about three weeks before Christmas that the specialities began to arrive: iced and decorated cakes; stuffed dates; candied fruits; boxes of fancy biscuits and sweets; sugared fancies; mixed nuts and valencia raisins. I needed neither the calendar nor the displays of tinsel and decorations in the shops to tell me Christmas was approaching. I could smell its all-pervading smell, rich and spicy and appetite-pricking.

As soon as the schools broke up for the holiday – even before they banded themselves together to go carol-singing – the children could be seen dancing eager attendance on greengrocers' shops, begging or buying two wooden hoops off fruit barrels to make their 'Christmas bush' which for most families was the substitute for a Christmas tree. The 'bush' was achieved by inserting one hoop through the other at right angles and decorating it with the tissue paper of different hues, cut into loops and with strands of tinsel. On Christmas Eve the bush was bedecked with baubles, small trinkets, sugar fancies, foil-wrapped neapolitans, apples and oranges, just as a tree would be, but then it was hung from the ceiling where, if the room were sufficiently airy, it provided a slowly revolving orb of colourful splendour.

Aunty Lizzie, who with her husband, Uncle Joe, shared Granny's home, was a gifted Christmas bush decorator and while other people rushed to trim their bushes last thing on Christmas Eve she was happy to spend several nights embellishing her own bush. First she collected as many different-coloured tissues as the shops could provide and after skilful cutting and ruching she attached the resulting frills to the hoops until she had achieved four miniature rainbows flamboyant enough to bring squeals of appreciation from visiting children. Both Aunty Lizzie and Granny loved Christmas and everything connected with the festival and though Uncle Joe was often on short time prior to the holiday, which meant they were short of money, they always contrived to bake dozens of mince pies and cakes and tarts in readiness for the family gathering on Christmas night.

Every year after Gran's party was over the family used to say to one another that there mustn't be another party next year. It was getting too much for Gran, they said. But every year when it came towards the end of November Aunty Lizzie announced, 'Gran says you're to make sure and come to the party at Christmas', and we always did make sure, and though Mother complained to Father when we got home that the parties were a fearful strain I always enjoyed myself immensely. One year, however, in early November Gran became ill. I thought I detected a note of satisfaction in Mother's voice when she told Father: 'It means there'll be no party this year.'

Father smiled obliquely. 'She'll get better in time for Christmas or die in the attempt,' he prophesied.

'I'll be glad of a quiet Christmas,' sighed Mother.

I felt dejected. Christmas at home was already too quiet for me and I could not imagine what it would be like without Gran's party. I willed her to recover in record time and pestered Aunty Lizzie to know if I could do anything to help. At last word came that Gran was able to get up, but with only two weeks to go to Christmas she was still having to rest for the greater part of the day.

When Aunty Lizzie came into the shop Mother said: 'You'll be relieved there's to be no party this year, I'm sure. It must make a lot of work for you.'

'We're having a party,' responded Aunty Lizzie with a triumphant gleam in her eye. 'Gran said so this morning.'

'She never did!' gasped Mother.

'She did,' affirmed Aunty Lizzie. 'She said it might be her last Christmas but she wants it to be a merry one.'

'But the work!' argued mother.

'Oh, she's going to trust me to do all the cooking,' replied Aunty Lizzie. 'She says so long as she can watch people enjoying themselves she's happy.'

Mother looked discomfited. She had convinced herself that this year she would have the quiet Christmas she yearned for and now it seemed Gran was going to be stubborn enough to deprive her of her rest. 'Well, we shan't come!' she exclaimed after a moment's hesitation. 'That means there'll be three less for you to have to cope with.'

I don't think Mother saw me glowering at her.

'She won't like that,' asserted Aunty Lizzie, who possibly suspected the reason for Mother's self-sacrifice. 'Anyway, what about Chipcart?'

'I'll come,' I piped up.

Mother gave me a quelling look. 'Chipcart can come perhaps but we shall stay at home. We couldn't bear to think we're putting a strain on you or on Gran so soon after her illness.' Mother sounded so virtuous I was almost taken in by her words and wondered, briefly, if I too ought to decline the invitation for Gran's sake.

It was again Aunty Lizzie who brought Granny's terse comment on Mother's apparent wish to defect from the annual family gatherings. 'If you don't want to come say so but if I'm well enough to ask you I'm well enough for you to come.'

'Well, I don't know whatever next,' said Mother exasperatedly. 'I suppose we'll have to humour her.'

As we had done every year since I could remember we set out in the chill dusk of Christmas day to walk to Gran's house and as always I ran ahead, eager to catch the first glimpse of the lighted windows of the parlour which signified that some of the family had already arrived. One knock and the door was opened by Gran herself, paler and shakier but with her face already crinkled in a radiant smile. While we embraced and wished one another a Merry Christmas and Aunty Lizzie took our coats and Father popped his walking stick into the decorated pottery holder the little Kelly lamp flickered as if nervous at the unaccustomed activity. We went into the kitchen where the big table was already set for tea and children were occupying the long sofa which had been pulled up to the table because there were not enough chairs for everyone. Squeezing in between the other children was for me part of the ritual of the feast, as was unfolding the poppy-flowered paper serviette and putting it beneath my plate in case I dropped crumbs on the starched white cloth. Gran's kitchen was a splendid place for parties, so bright and cheerful it seemed as if the colour and spirit of Christmas lingered there throughout the year. The big stove was, in winter or summer, aglow with the reflection of busy flames; the rosebud-pattern china on the alcove shelves was always lustrous and the red paisley-patterned cushions and covers reminded one of the colour of Santa Claus's cloak. The walls were patterned too and hung with ornaments: a white china cornucopia; a red glass half-yard of ale that looked like an outsize pipe; a yellow glass germ stick that resembled a long piece of barley sugar and had to be wiped clean of germs every day; pearl-inlaid trays depicting scenes of Japanese life, and a glass dome that contained shells and coloured seaweeds from some tropical country. There were pictures too, of children crossing a farmyard and being chased by geese; of Lord Roberts, his uniform brimful of medals; and there was a framed collection of hand-embroidered valentines which Gran had collected during the Boer War and which I loved to be allowed to admire at close quarters.

When tea was over the trinkets and sweets from the Christmas bush were distributed among the children; the women washed dishes in the back kitchen and the men produced pipes and cigarettes and lit them with spills ignited in the fire. There was always a plentiful supply of spills on the hob at Granny's, thanks to Uncle Joe who spent his Sunday mornings cutting them, and except for lighting the fire each day matches were never used. Someone noticed that Granny was becoming agitated because, she said, the gas was flaring above the mantle and there was a tetchy moment while Uncle Joe, who was very short-sighted, stood on a chair and adjusted the light by pulling first one chain and then the other in compliance with the many directions he received. There was gaslight in only the kitchen at Granny's and as she was still inclined to regard it with awe it was usually turned low for safety.

As soon as the women had finished the dishes and taken off their borrowed aprons everyone, except Granny, who was too frail, and Aunty Lizzie, who was too busy, joined in games like 'Hunt the Slipper', 'Consequences', and 'Passing the Ring'. Ginger wine was produced for the children and a bottle of port wine for the adults, which no doubt helped to increase the fervour of their voices when the brass lantern clock showed a quarter to nine and we all moved into the parlour for a sing-song round the harmonium. The Christmas party always ended with a sing-song and the sing-song always ended with Granny's favourite hymn; old and young joined in singing 'The day Thou gavest, Lord, is ended' to the audience of glass pigs on the mantelpiece, while Granny relaxed in her armchair, nodding and smiling on us with pride and satisfaction.

We put on our outdoor clothes, said our goodbyes and went out into the frost-cold silent street. Father set a jaunty pace for the walk home to which I hummed one of the songs we had been singing earlier.

As soon as we reached our own house mother went straight to the living room and sagged into her chair.

'I'm jiggered,' she complained. 'I felt roasted all evening.'

'It does get hot,' agreed Father.

'Well, I hope there won't be a party next year, that's all,' she said fretfully.

Father looked at her steadily for a moment and then turned away. 'There's only one way there won't be a party,' he said pointedly, 'and after all, she's your mother.'

from
Whatever Happened to Tom Mix?

TED WILLIS

*Ted Willis, a prolific playwright for radio and television over many years, is perhaps best known as the creator of **Dixon of Dock Green**, the long-running TV series starring Jack Warner as the avuncular local police sergeant. Lord Willis himself was brought up in the Depression years in a working-class household, and in his autobiography **Whatever Happened to Tom Mix?** he looks back on the Christmas celebrations of those difficult times.*

(Tom Mix was a well-known star of cowboy films in the 1920s and 1930s, and therefore represents for Ted Willis the departed years of childhood).

It was possible to trace the progress of Christmas Day by the succession of attractive smells which invaded our house like so many invisible but welcome gatecrashers.

Early in the morning, long before the church bells started to ring or the light to break, we groped our way towards the socks and stockings which my mother had stuffed with sweets, oranges and other trifles and set at the foot of the bed. There would be parcels too – containing nothing very expensive or very elaborate – and if curiosity were stronger than appetite, we would open these first. But before long, we would attack the little soft-skinned tangerines which we knew we should find in the stockings, and the sharp, pungent scent of orange drifted through the house . . .

By mid-morning a new combination of smells filled the house. Turkey was never on our Christmas menu in those days, but there was always a piece of beef or pork, together with a chicken – all bought at the tail-end of Christmas Eve when the prices were at a knockdown level.

If we had a crowd of relatives coming for Christmas dinner, it was possible that the joint plus the chicken might be too big to be accommodated in my mother's oven, for there was the inevitable Yorkshire pudding to be cooked, as well as roast potatoes, and mince pies. In this event, for a copper or two, old Mr Hamilton would roast the meats in his bakery oven, a complication which made the cooking of the dinner a matter of meticulous timing. My mother, helped by sister Nell, managed it somehow.

When everything was ready, the kitchen table was pulled out, and short pieces of planking or the boards from my mother's old wooden mangle were placed in position from chair to chair, to make extra seating. If there was no room in the kitchen, two or three children had to be seated in the scullery, to eat their dinner off the mangle-boards which were set up at the mangle itself.

When the first – and main – course was demolished, the aroma of cooked meat and fowl receded, to be replaced by the spicy odour of Christmas pudding and mince pies. These were always home made, concocted from flour, eggs, sugar, dried fruit, candied peel, spices and other beautiful things, which were all mixed and stirred in big earthenware bowls at regular pre-Christmas kitchen ceremonies. At those ceremonies it was considered good luck for each of us to take the wooden spoon, make a wish, and stir the mixture. There was great competition to secure the lumps of hard sugar left from the candied peel, or to lick round the bowl when the mixture had been removed.

The pudding and pies were always eaten with hot, smooth, custard. We set upon this with unabated energy and enthusiasm, but within minutes the pressure of the food we'd already eaten began to take its toll, and the pace slackened. By the time we pushed our plates away, we were painfully full, our stomachs skin-tight, and for the next hour or so there was a steady procession towards the back yard.

After a slow, sluggish afternoon, the day began to break into a renewed canter with the arrival of evening and more relatives and friends. Now the bitter smell of ale and stout invaded the house as bottles were brought in from the pubs and the adults set about the serious business of drinking. Apart from our own crowd, the Hares would have their own Christmas party upstairs, and there were times when the ceilings sagged under their weight, while our china clinked and swung to the rhythm of their dancing, and flakes of plaster floated down like grey snow.

As the night wore on, the adults grew more and more raucous, while the children became tired and irritable. We were exiled to the kitchen to play among ourselves, but such games usually ended in quarrels. My mother's patience was wearing thin by this time, but she would make one more heroic effort to hold her temper in. Putting her hands on her hips in a gesture that was half-threat, half-appeal, she would say:

'Now, behave yourselves, behave yourselves! You don't want a good hiding on Christmas Day, do you? Because that's what you'll get!'

At last the younger ones were put to bed, where, in spite of the rising noise from the front room, they slept the sleep of sheer exhaustion; the older ones were allowed to join the adults for a little while, sitting heavy-eyed in the corners watching the strange behaviour and stranger games of their elders.

from
A Child's Christmas in Wales

DYLAN THOMAS

Dylan Thomas was one of the century's great individualists – unconventional, frequently drunk, respecter of nobody, and a wizard with words. Childhood was a theme which recurred over and over again in his work, and memories of his own childhood in Swansea in the 1920s form the basis of his humorous and lively story **A Child's Christmas in Wales** *(published posthumously in 1954), whose language fizzles and flashes with the brilliance of a firecracker.*

Mistletoe hung from the gas brackets in all the front parlours; there was sherry and walnuts and bottled beer and crackers by the dessertspoons; and cats in their fur-abouts watched the fires; and the high-heaped fire spat, all ready for the chestnuts and the mulling pokers.

Some few large men sat in the front parlours, without their collars, Uncles almost certainly, trying their new cigars, holding them out judiciously at arms' length, returning them to their mouths, coughing, then holding them out again as though waiting for the explosion; and some few small Aunts, not wanted in the kitchen, nor anywhere else for that matter, sat on the very edges of their chairs, poised and brittle, afraid to break, like faded cups and saucers.

Not many those mornings trod the piling streets: an old man always, fawn-bowlered, yellow-gloved and, at this time of year, with spats of snow, would take his constitutional to the white bowling green and back, as he would take it wet or fine on Christmas Day or Doomsday; sometimes two hale young men, with big pipes blazing, no overcoats and wind-blown scarfs, would trudge, unspeaking, down to the forlorn sea, to work up an appetite, to blow away the fumes, who knows, to walk into the waves until nothing of them was left but the two curling smoke clouds of their inextinguishable briars. Then I would be slap-dashing home, the gravy smell of the dinners of others, the bird smell, the brandy, the

125

pudding and mince, coiling up to my nostrils, when out of a snow-clogged side lane would come a boy the spit of myself, with a pink-tipped cigarette and the violet past of a black eye, cocky as a bullfinch, leering all to himself.

I hated him on sight and sound, and would be about to put my dog whistle to my lips and blow him off the face of Christmas when suddenly he, with a violet wink, put *his* whistle to *his* lips and blew so stridently, so high, so exquisitely loud, that gobbling faces, their cheeks bulged with goose, would press against their tinselled windows, the whole length of the white echoing street.

For dinner we had turkey and blazing pudding, and after dinner the Uncles sat in front of the fire, loosened all buttons, put their large moist hands over their watch chains, groaned a little and slept. Mothers, aunts and sisters scuttled to and fro, bearing tureens. Auntie Bessie, who had already been frightened, twice, by a clock-work mouse, whimpered at the sideboard and had some elderberry wine. The dog was sick. Auntie Dosie had to have three aspirins, but Auntie Hannah, who liked port, stood in the middle of the snowbound back yard, singing like a big-bosomed thrush. I would blow up balloons to see how big they would blow up to; and, when they burst, which they all did, the Uncles jumped and rumbled. In the rich and heavy afternoon, the Uncles breathing like dolphins and the snow descending, I would sit among festoons and Chinese lanterns and nibble dates and try to make a model man-o'-war, following the Instructions for Little Engineers, and produce what might be mistaken for a sea-going tramcar.

40

Albert and the Liner

KEITH WATERHOUSE

*Keith Waterhouse's best writing never departs far in its subject matter from the northern England of the 30s, 40s and 50s which he knew as a child and as a reporter on a Yorkshire newspaper. The urge to write seems to have been with him from an early age: when he was ten he wrote a paper called the **Daily Treasure**, and took advantage of his job as a paper-boy to deliver his news-sheet to unsuspecting readers wrapped up in copies of the **Yorkshire Post**. There Is a Happy Land (1957) and **Billy Liar** (1959) were the first of a string of successful novels, and the beginning of a writing career which broadened out to include material for radio, television, the stage and the cinema.*

*   **Albert and the Liner** is set in familiar Waterhouse territory, a northern town in the Depression years, with its City Arcade and trams, and the story is marvellously evocative of that period, with its nostalgic references to Felix the Cat, 'Film Fun' annuals, Meccano models, and Dinky toys.*

Below the military striking clock in the City Arcade there was, and for all I know still is, a fabulous toyshop.

It was a magic grotto, that shop. A zoo, a circus, a pantomime, a travelling show, a railway exhibition, an enchanted public library, a clockwork museum, an archive of boxed games, a pavilion of sports equipment, a depository of all the joys of the indefinite, endless leisure of the winter holiday – but first, the military striking clock.

Once a year we were taken to see the clock strike noon – an event in our lives as colourful, and traditional, and as fixed and immovable in the calendar of pageantry as Trooping the Colour. Everybody who was anybody assembled, a few minutes before twelve, on the patch of worn tiles incorporating an advertisement for tomato sausages done in tasteful mosaic, beneath that military striking clock.

There was me, and Jack Corrigan, and the crippled lad from No 43, and there was even Albert Skinner – whose father never took him anywhere, not even to the Education Office to explain why he'd been playing truant.

Albert Skinner, with his shaved head and his shirt-lap hanging out of his trousers, somehow attached himself, insinuated himself, like a stray dog. You'd be waiting at the tram stop with your mother, all dolled up in your Sunday clothes for going into town and witnessing the ceremony of the military striking clock, and Albert, suddenly, out of nowhere, would be among those present.

'Nah, then, kid.'

And your mother, out of curiosity, would say – as she was meant to say – 'You're never going into town looking like that, are you, Albert?'

And Albert would say: 'No. I was, only I've lost my tram fare.'

And your mother, out of pity, would say – as she was meant to say – 'Well, you can come with us. But you'll have to tidy yourself up. Tuck your shirt in, Albert.'

So at Christmastime Albert tagged on to see the military striking clock strike noon. After the mechanical soldiers of the King had trundled back into their plaster-of-Paris garrison, he, with the rest of us, was allowed to press his nose to the fabulous toyshop window.

Following a suitable period of meditation, we were then treated to a bag of mint imperials – *'and think on, they're to share between you'* – and conveyed home on the rattling tram. And there, thawing out our mottled legs by the fireside, we were supposed to compose our petitions to Father Christmas.

Dear Father Christmas, for Christmas I would like . . .

'Don't know what to put,' we'd say at length to one another, seeking some kind of corporate inspiration.

'Why don't you ask him for a sledge? I am.'

'Barmpot, what do you want a sledge for? What if it doesn't snow?'

'Well – a cricket bat and stumps, and that.'

'Don't play cricket at Christmas, barmpot.'

Albert Skinner said nothing. Nobody, in fact, said anything worth saying, during those tortured hours of voluntary composition.

With our blank jumbo jotters on our knees, we would suck our copying-ink pencils until our tongues turned purple – but it wasn't that we were short of ideas. Far from it: sledges, cricket bats with stumps and that, fountain pens, dynamos, cinematographs complete with Mickey Mouse films – the fact of the matter was, there was too much choice.

For the fabulous toyshop, which sparked off our exotic and finally blank imaginations, was the nearest thing on this earth to Santa's Workshop. It was like a bankruptcy sale in heaven. The big clockwork train ran clockwise and the small electric train ran anti-clockwise, and there was Noah's Ark, and a tram conductor's set, and a junior typewriter revolving on a brightly-lit glass shelf, and a fairy cycle hanging from the ceiling on invisible wires, and a tin steam roller, and the Tip-Top Annual and the Film Fun Annual and the Radio Fun Annual and the Jingles Annual and the Joker Annual and the Jester Annual, and board games, and chemistry sets, and conjuring sets, and carpentry sets – everything, in short, that the modern boy would give his eye-teeth for.

Everything that Albert Skinner would have given his eye-teeth for, in fact, and much that Albert Skinner would never get. And not only him. There were items that no reasonable modern boy expected to find in his Christmas pillow-case – not even though he bartered every tooth in his head and promised to be a good lad till kingdom come.

The centrepiece of the fabulous toyshop's window display was always something out of the reach of ordinary mortals, such as the Blackpool Tower in Meccano, or a mechanical carousel with horses that went up and down on their brass poles like the real thing, or Windsor Castle made of a million building bricks, or Buckingham Palace with nobs on – flood-lit. None of us had to be told that such luxuries were beyond Father Christmas's price range.

This year the window featured a splendid model of the *Queen Mary*, which had recently been launched on Clydebank. It was about four feet long, with real lights in the portholes, real steam curling out of the funnels, and a crew, and passengers, and life-boats, and cabin trunks, all to scale – and clearly it was not for the likes of us.

Having seen it and marvelled at it, we dismissed this expensive dream from our minds, sucked our copying-ink pencils and settled down to list our prosaic requests – for Plasticine, for farmyard animals that poisoned you when you licked the paint off, and for one pair of roller skates between two of us.

All of us, that is to say, except Albert Skinner. Having considered several possibilities, and taken advice on the rival merits of a racing track with eight electric sports cars and a glove puppet of Felix the Cat he'd rather fancied, Albert calmly announced that he'd given thought to all our suggestions and he was asking Father Christmas for the *Queen Mary*.

This, as you might imagine, was greeted with some scepticism.

'What – that one in the Arcade window? With the lights and the steam coming out and that? You've never asked for that, have you?'

'Yeh – course I have. Why shouldn't I?'

'He's blinking crackers. Hey, Skinno, why don't you ask for them soldiers that march in and out and bang that clock? Because you've more chance of getting them than that *Queen Mary*.'

'If I'd wanted them soldiers I'd have asked for them. Only I don't. So I've asked him for the *Queen Mary*.'

'Who – Father Christmas?'

'No – him on the Quaker Oats Box, who do you think?'

'Bet you haven't, man. Bet you're having us on.'

'I'm not – God's honour. I've asked him for the *Queen Mary*.'

'Let's see the letter, then.'

'Can't – I've chucked it up the chimney.'

'Yeh – bet you have. Anyway, your dad won't get it for you – he can't afford it.'

'What's it got to do with him? I'm asking Father Stinking Rotten Christmas for it, not me dad. Dozy.'

'What else have you asked for, Skinno?'

'Nowt. I don't want owt else. I just want the *Queen Mary*. And I'm getting it, as well.'

Little else was said at the time, but privately we thought Albert was a bit of an optimist. For one thing, the *Queen Mary* was so big and so grand and so lit-up that it was probably not even for sale. For another, we were all well aware that Father Christmas's representative in the Skinner household was a sullen, foul-tempered collier who also happened to be unemployed.

Albert's birthday present, it was generally known, had been a pair of boots – instead of the scooter on which, at that time, he had set his heart.

Even so, Albert continued to insist that he was getting the *Queen Mary* for Christmas. 'Ask my dad,' he would say. 'If you don't believe me, ask my dad.'

None of us cared to broach the subject with the excitable Mr Skinner. But sometimes, when we went to his house to swop comics, Albert would raise the matter himself.

'Dad, I am, aren't I? Aren't I, Dad? Getting that *Queen Mary* for Christmas?'

Mr Skinner, dourly whittling a piece of wood by the fireside after the habit of all the local miners, would growl without looking up: 'You'll get a clout over the bloody earhole if you don't stop chelping.'

Albert would turn complacently to us. 'I am, see. I'm getting the *Queen Mary*. Aren't I, Dad? Dad? Aren't I?'

Sometimes, when his father had come home from the pub in a bad mood (which was quite often), Albert's pleas for reassurance would be met with a more vicious response. 'Will you shut up about the bloody Queen swining Mary!' Mr Skinner would shout. 'You gormless little git, do you think I'm made of money?'

Outside, his ear tingling from the blow his father had landed on it, Albert would bite back the tears and declare stubbornly: 'I'm still getting it. You wait till Christmas.'

Christmas Eve was but a fortnight off by then. Most of us had a shrewd idea, from hints dropped by our mothers, what Father Christmas would be bringing us – or, in most cases, not bringing. 'I don't think Father Christmas can manage an electric train set this year, our Terry. He says they're too expensive. He says he might be able to find you a tip-up lorry.'

Being realists, we accepted our lowly position on Father Christmas's scale of priorities – and we tried our best to persuade Albert to accept his.

'You're not *forced* to get that *Queen Mary*, you know, Skinno.'

'Who says I'm not?'

'My mam. She says it's too big to go in Father Christmas's sack.'

'Yeh, well that's all *she* knows. Because he's fetching Jacky Corrigan a fairy cycle – so if he can't get the *Queen Mary* in his sack, how can he get a stinking rotten fairy cycle?'

'Yeh, well he isn't fetching me a fairy cycle at all, clever-clogs, he's fetching me a John Bull printing outfit. 'Cos he told my mam.'

'I don't care what he told her, or what he didn't tell her. He's still fetching me that *Queen Mary*.'

The discussion was broken up by the sudden appearance of Mr Skinner at their scullery window. 'If I hear one more bloody word from you about that bloody *Queen Mary*, you'll get nothing for Christmas! Do you hear me?' And there the matter rested.

A few days later the crippled lad at No 43 was taken by the Church Ladies Guild to see the military striking clock in the City

Arcade, and when he came home he reported that the model of the *Queen Mary* was no longer in the window of the fabulous toyshop.

'I know,' said Albert, having confirmed that his father was out of earshot. 'I'm getting it for Christmas.'

And indeed, it seemed the only explanation possible. The fabulous toyshop never changed its glittering display until after Boxing Day – it was unheard of. Some minor item might vanish out of the window – the Noah's Ark, perhaps, or a farmyard, or a game of Monopoly or two. There was a rational explanation for this: Father Christmas hadn't enough toys to go round and he'd been obliged, so to speak, to call on his sub-contractors. But the set-piece, the Blackpool Tower made out of Meccano or the carousel with the horses that went round and round and up and down – that was never removed; never. And yet the *Queen Mary* had gone. What had happened? Had Father Christmas gone mad? Had Mr Skinner bribed him – and if so, with what? Had Mr Skinner won the football pools? Or was it that Albert's unswerving faith could move mountains – not to mention ocean-going liners with real steam and real lights in the portholes? Or was it, as one cynic among us insisted, that the *Queen Mary* had been privately purchased for some pampered grammar school lad on the posher side of town?

'You just wait and see,' said Albert.

And then it was Christmas morning; and after the chocolate pennies had been eaten and all the kitchens in the street were awash with nut-shells and orange peel, we all flocked out to show off our presents – sucking our brand-new torches to make our cheeks glow red, or brandishing a lead soldier or two in the pretence that we had a whole regiment of them indoors. Those who had wanted wooden forts were delighted with their painting books; those who had prayed for electric racing cars were content with their Dinky toys; those who had asked for roller skates were happy with their pencil boxes; and there was no sign of Albert.

No one, in fact, expected to see him at all. But just as we were asking each other what Father Christmas could have brought him – a new jersey, perhaps, or a balaclava helmet – he came bounding, leaping, jumping, almost somersaulting into the street. 'I've got it! I've got it! I've got it!'

Painting books and marbles and games of Happy Families were abandoned in the gutter as we clustered around Albert, who was cradling in his arms what seemed on first inspection to be a length of wood. Then we saw that it had been roughly carved at both ends, to make a bow and stern, and that three cotton-reels had been nailed to it for funnels. A row of tin-tacks marked the Plimsoll line, and there were stuck-on bits of cardboard for the portholes. The whole thing was painted over in sticky lamp-black, except for the lettering on the portside.

'*The Queen Mary*,' it said. In white, wobbling letters. Capital T, small h, capital E. Capital Q, small u, capital E, capital E, small n. Capital M, small a, capital R, small y. Penmanship had never been Mr Skinner's strong point.

'See!' crowed Albert complacently. 'I told you he'd fetch me it, and he's fetched me it.'

Our grunts of appreciation, though somewhat strained, were genuine enough. Albert's *Queen Mary* was a crude piece of work, but clearly many hours of labour, and much love, had gone into it. Its clumsy contours alone must have taken night after night of whittling by the fireside.

Mr Skinner, pyjama-jacket tucked into his trousers, had come out of the house and was standing by his garden gate. Albert, in a rush of happiness, ran to his father and flung his arms around him and hugged him. Then he waved the *Queen Mary* on high.

'Look, Dad! Look what I've got for Christmas! Look what Father Christmas has fetched me! You knew he would, didn't you, all this time!'

'Get out of it, you soft little bugger,' said Mr Skinner. He drew contentedly on his empty pipe, cuffed Albert over the head as a matter of habit, and went indoors.

41

African Christmas

JOHN PRESS

The unusual experience, for an Englishman, of celebrating Christmas in tropical heat was the stimulus for John Press's poem. During the war he served in the Royal Artillery, mainly in East Africa, and the verses printed here recall a Christmas in Mombasa, where December is usually the hottest time of the year. After the war John Press joined the British Council and went on to hold appointments in, among other places, Athens, Salonika, Madras and Colombo.

Here are no signs of festival,
No holly and no mistletoe,
No robin and no crackling fire,
And no soft, feathery fall of snow.

In England one could read the words
Telling how shepherds in the fold
Followed the star and reached the barn
Which kept the Saviour from the cold,

And picture in one's mind the scene –
The tipsy, cheerful foreign troops,
The kindly villagers who stood
About the Child in awkward groups.

But in this blazing Christmas heat
The ox, the ass, the bed of hay
The shepherds and the Holy Child
Are stilted figures in a play.

Exiles, we see that we, like slaves
To symbol and to memory,
Have worshipped, not the incarnate Christ,
But tinsel on the Christmas tree.

42

from
The GIs

NORMAN LONGMATE

*When the USA entered the Second World War in December 1941 and large numbers of American troops began to arrive in England, it soon became apparent that there was a culture clash between the two countries. The American authorities went to great lengths, with propaganda films and information leaflets, to prepare the members of their armed forces for some of the differences they would find in England, and although the jibe about the Americans being 'over-paid, over-sexed and over here' was current in some quarters, in the main the trans-Atlantic troops were accepted and welcomed by the majority of people in this country. Christmas was a particularly important time, as everyone thought about relatives and loved ones far away, and it provided a perfect opportunity for English and Americans to come together in mutual celebration as described here by the historian Norman Longmate in an extract from **The GIs**, his exhaustively researched and very readable book about the American presence in this country during the war.*

With its combination of good fellowship, sentiment and generosity Christmas was an occasion made for the GIs and many British people still remember the lavish presents they received. One woman, then in her teens and living near Aintree, recalls a Christmas visitor who 'came with a gift for each member of the family . . . He gave my father a box of fifty cigars . . . something beyond his wildest dreams,' and 'whilst with us . . . sat down and wrote to his "mom"', with the result that 'Mom wrote to us expressing her gratitude and sent three enormous food parcels and continued to send them right through until the end of rationing'. An air force Sergeant radio operator from Optima, Oklahoma, remembers a typical invitation for Christmas 1942 to spend the holiday with his 'buddy' at the Alperton home of the latter's girl friend. 'We got a forty-eight-hour pass and . . . ten pounds of sugar and three large cans of peaches from our Mess Sergeant,' he remembers. Their hosts seemed 'well pleased' with these gifts, as well they might be: the sugar ration at this time was eight ounces a week and tinned fruit was unobtainable.

135

A woman then living with her parents in Stilton, Huntingdonshire, recalls the similar bounty which descended upon them, even more unexpectedly, one Christmas Eve. 'We heard a knock on our front door and when we went to answer it there was no one there, but a huge kitbag full of presents on the step, which the GIs had left us in appreciation of my mother doing their washing. There was butter and cheese in tins, chocolate and rich cakes and games and toys. My young brother asked if Father Christmas had been and my mother said, "Yes, in GI clothing".' 'Right up to the time when I finally decided that there was no Father Christmas,' remembers the granddaughter of a Norfolk publican – four when the GIs arrived and seven when they left – 'I believed that he chewed gum, spoke with an American accent . . . and called all little girls "honey".'

'The event I remember above all was the Christmas Party. It was December 1942. Every child in the school was invited – including all the evacuees from London – and we were collected from the village green in a fleet of army lorries – quite a thrill for children more used to horses and carts. The party was held in the large dining hall. The hall was decorated with tall Christmas trees hung all over with silver streamers. The food was all set out on little tables – sandwiches, biscuits, and cakes with fruit juice to drink. The sandwiches were rather disappointing as they all seemed to be made with peanut butter. I hated peanut butter. There was also meat spread with what I took to be strawberry jam, but must have been cranberry sauce. Father Christmas duly arrived, in a Spitfire and no one mentioned reindeer – and handed out parcels of sweets and biscuits to each child . . . To end off we all had a filmshow; mostly Donald Duck and Mickey Mouse, and then home again in the lorries. It was the only party I went to for a long time and I have never forgotten it.'

A Spitfire was not the only unfamiliar form of transport which Father Christmas adopted between 1942 and 1944. *The Stars and Stripes* recorded one party where, rather curiously, the old gentleman having crowned his traditional red robes and beard with a steel helmet, had arrived by B-17, but his favourite vehicle was a jeep. One landgirl working near Faringdon in Berkshire, remembers a draw among the NCOs of a local cavalry regiment for the right to play Santa Claus and the winner came back proud of his Cockney accent: the guests had been evacuees from London. Even braver were twelve Sergeants from the air force station at Honington in West Suffolk, who distributed 'candy' at the local Dr Barnardo's Home by piling twelve large dishes with sweets, standing 'in the middle of the boys in the large dining hall and shouting "Come and get it!"' The episode proved a great success. 'The Sergeants disappeared on to the floor under the onslaught' but 'eventually emerged triumphant, although somewhat dishevelled.'

1944

This was the Christmas which everyone had expected to be the first of peacetime. It proved instead the last, and grimmest, of the war. In the Ardennes von Rundstedt's offensive had revealed that the Germans were not beaten yet and an icy belt of snow and fog lay over much of Western Europe, although above England the skies were, for once, clear. The black-out, with the capture of the German airfields in France, had given way to a 'dim-out' and the daughter of one Suffolk rector remembers, as a sign of things to come, seeing the B-17s that Christmas Eve climbing into the darkness in their hundreds with their lights on, no doubt to carry supplies to hungry, shivering Europe. 'I was walking through a white frosted park when they were going out,' she remembers, recalling 'the incredible beauty of the sky, lighting up the trees which were heavy with frost, and the snow, was a sight that became a great comfort to me.' A little later that evening another young woman who helped her parents to run the village shop at Mulfords Hill, within the perimeter of the great American camp at Aldermaston, near Reading, went to the door to see off a group of GIs who had come for supper. 'There had been a fall of snow,' she remembers, 'which had frozen on the trees making icicles . . . The air was crisp and the hoar frost glistened in the moonlight.' The family had asked their guests to return for Christmas dinner next day, and the GIs had promised: 'You'll be hearing from us soon.' The family learned what they meant when awakened at midnight by the sound of music coming over the tannoy. It was 'Christians Awake', followed by 'Silent Night' sung as a solo by one of their recent guests, a unique and public Christmas greeting.

from
Village Diary

'MISS READ'

'Miss Read' is the pseudonym of a school teacher who turned to writing after the Second World War, and from the mid-1950s wrote prolifically, producing almost a book a year. Her teaching experience is evident in this description of Christmas preparations at the junior school of Fairacre, the imaginary village whose year is chronicled in her book **Village Diary** *(1957).*

Preparations for Christmas are now in full swing. For weeks past the shops in Caxley have been a blaze of coloured lights and decorated with Father Christmases, decked trees, silver balls and all the other paraphernalia. Even our grocer's shop in Fairacre has cotton-wool snow, hanging on threads, down the window, and this, and the crib already set up in the church all add to the children's enchantment.

It has turned bitterly cold, with a cruel east wind, which has scattered the last of the leaves and ruffles the feathers of the birds who sit among the bare branches. The Tortoise[1] stoves are kept roaring away, but nothing can cure the fiendish draught from the sky-light above my desk, and the one from the door, where generations of feet have worn the lintel into a hollow.

Yesterday afternoon the whole school was busy making Christmas decorations and Christmas cards. There is nothing that children like more than making brightly-coloured paper chains, and their tongues wagged happily as the paste brushes were plied, and yet another glowing link was added to the festoons that lay piled on the floor. All this glory grows so deliciously quickly and the knowledge that, very soon, it will be swinging aloft, above their heads, among the pitch-pine rafters – an enchanting token of all the joys that

---

[1]A cast-iron stove for heating large buildings; see page 145.

Christmas holds in store – makes them work with more than usual energy.

In Miss Jackson's room the din was terrific, so excited were the chain-makers. The only quiet group here was the one which was composed of about eight small children who had elected to crayon Christmas cards instead. Among them was the little Pratt boy. I stopped to admire his effort. His picture was of a large and dropsical robin, with the fiercest of red breasts, and very small and inadequate legs, as there was only a quarter of an inch of space left at the bottom for these highly-necessary appendages. His face was solemn with the absorption of the true artist.

'It's for Miss Bunce,' he told me. 'You knows – the one at Barrisford what took me to the hostipple to have my eye done. She writes to me ever so often, and sometimes sends me sweets. D'you reckon she'll like it?'

He held up his masterpiece and surveyed it anxiously at arm's length.

I told him truthfully that I was sure she would like it very much, and that all sensible people liked robins on Christmas cards. With a sigh of infinite satisfaction he replaced it on the desk, and prepared to face the horrid intricacies of writing 'HAPPY CHRISTMAS' inside.

44

I've Had a Lousy Xmas

ROGER McGOUGH

In the 1960s, largely as a result of the success of the Beatles, Liverpool became the centre of Britain's pop culture (the American poet Allen Ginsberg even claimed that it was 'the centre of the consciousness of the human universe'). Although a large proportion of this culture was musical, there was also a resurgence of poetry, written in a direct, immediate style that appealed to a much wider audience than poetry usually commanded at that time. Roger McGough, whose work is represented here, was one of the leading names in this movement.

I have had a lousy Xmas
I have had enough of chickens' legs
    and breasts and parsons' noses
    of mistletoe and white draining-board sandwiches.
I have raped a packet of 'pleasurable Players'
    (to symphonic accompaniment)
    and have drunk
    five million bottles of Guinness
    (daily).

I have had a lousy Xmas
I have driven a tinfoil turkey
    through the jolly, hollied streets of Liverpool
    shouting: 'Get stuffed'
    to the plum-duffed little people
    the mince-pied
    pie-eyed little people
    dying in their decorated parlours.

I've Had a Lousy Xmas

I have had a lousy Xmas
I have received presents
   from all my enemies:
   a portrait of the Queen
   back copies of *Encounter* and *London Magazine*
   a bar of Lifebuoy toilet soap
   a gamekeeper's outfit
   and an LP of this poem.

At tea on Boxing Day
I pulled a cracker
   and out popped dead North Vietnamese
   and South Vietnamese
   and I wept
   into my trifle.

I have had a lousy Xmas
   because I believe in Santa Claus
   and someone's gone
   and crucified him.

45

from
The Solitary Landscape

EDWARD STOREY

*The poet Edward Storey has his roots deep in the Fen country of eastern England, and has written a number of books describing what this rather bleak, overwhelmingly flat part of the world means to him. In **The Solitary Landscape** (1975) a Christmas Eve drive from his home in Peterborough into neighbouring Northamptonshire, and the following Christmas Day celebrations with his family, prompt his remembrances of Christmases past.*

Now

Not a star moves out of place. Orion is as constant in its distance and form as it has been since Man gave names to constellations. The air is clear enough for us to see the Pleiades and nearer reaches of the Milky Way. The sky is silent. No hint of echoes from beyond the space that separates the stars. On earth the fields are dark with darker shapes of trees. And village lights, like stars caught in the grass, give meaning to the miles we travel through.

The city is left behind. We pass the villages of Orton Longueville, Orton Waterville, Alwalton and Chesterton. In the distance is Fotheringhay and its royal church. We cannot see it but we know it's there. It's all part of the history we feel on roads that knew a certain tragedy or fame four centuries ago. We mention every village tucked between those spaces on the earth and hidden now beyond the waiting dark. It's all so familiar. The earth and sky. And yet tonight it has this annual significance when out of the fixed and ordinary things we look for miracles. If a star did move, if sounds were to come from the sky, we'd tremble and be terrified. But because nothing unusual happens we drive on in a world of our own towards the ancient town of Oundle and The Talbot Hotel for our Christmas Eve dinner.

Arriving out of the country dark into the brightness of the town the lights hurt our eyes, the streets bring us back to reality. Cars are

142

parked outside the hotel. The bars are crowded. The inn, appropriately, is full. The dining-room is warm and candle-lit. Tables steam with good food. Glasses glow with wine. Surely the statisticians can't be right about half the world starving! Not on Christmas Eve? So who's got it wrong?

The conscience is consoled by words like, 'But what can you do about it now? After all, you're not making a pig of yourself.' No, but the thought was there, as uncomfortable as a stab of indigestion half-way through the second course. And only our wish to be quiet on Christmas Eve and away from all the last-minute panic in the city redeems the deed. Here, in a public place, it is surprisingly easy to be private and alone, to find the time to ponder over some of the values and memories. To feel gratitude and contentment.

We drive back through the silent countryside – Southwick, Woodnewton, Nassington, Wansford, Southorpe and Ufford. The roads twist between hedges and stone walls, past cottages and rooms where children sleep with presents now at the foot of their beds. On this one night of the year it all has to be true . . .

The villages wait. The fields remain dark. And not a star moves out of place. Not a sound comes from the sky.

As It Was

After a quiet Christmas Eve I still have what is, I suppose, an old-fashioned Christmas, spending Christmas Day at the home of my parents with other members of the family. Sometimes there can be fourteen of us gathered round the table and each year the same games are played, the same stories told, the same memories brought out like the carols, decorations and nut-crackers to give the season its customary pattern. And always other Christmases come back into our thoughts and conversations. When I watch my six-year-old nephew, David, I see quite clearly those Christmas Days I had when I was a child his age. The mystery of the old man with a red cloak and a white beard who somehow squeezed down our chimney with a sack of toys ceased to be a mystery in the morning when the bottom of the bed was loaded with presents. The thrill of waking early and rushing into my parents' bedroom with some of the toys, the excitement of going downstairs into a room that had been transformed during the night with a Christmas tree and coloured lights, the very taste of the home-made pork pie we had for breakfast, all come back to me as I see myself in this other child . . .

By the time breakfast was over the day was really alive. The radio would be loud with 'Christians Awake' or 'O Come all ye faithful' and final preparations for our Christmas Dinner would put the small kitchen out of bounds as far as the children were concerned. Toy cannons shot down a troop of cavalrymen, a new fire-engine crashed into the piano, and happy shouts came from every part of the house. Into this confusion of noise, colour, crackers, balloons and humming-tops came my grandparents to spend their Christmas quietly with us.

No one bothered how much coal or wood was put on the fire. The room just grew hotter and hotter. One year the paper decorations caught fire and all the balloons burst. There was a great fanning of arms and towels and stamping of feet. The room filled with a grey cloud of smoke that spread into a black snowstorm and I rushed out into the yard shouting 'Fire! Fire!'. There was no one to hear me. The neighbours were involved in their own fires. The forlorn white world outside looked cold and desolate. Only the birds had life as they pecked away at a few scraps that had been thrown out for them. They did not even look up as I waved my arms in an abortive attempt to raise the alarm. The sky was as expressionless as a frozen pond. The old wash-house at the bottom of the garden looked far away and forsaken. The water-tap was frozen and a long icicle hung there gnarled and white as candle-wax.

When my mother called me back into the house the panic was over. The smoke was disappearing through the open window and I could see quite clearly now the unperturbed outlines of the china dogs on the mantelpiece and the untroubled face of the wall clock. From the ceiling hung the wire skeletons of Chinese lanterns and the charred pieces of tape on which the balloons had blossomed.

'Would you like a game of draughts?' asked my grandmother, as if nothing had happened, 'or Snakes and Ladders?'

46

Christmas

JOHN BETJEMAN

Sir John Betjeman's stature as a poet was recognized officially in 1972, when he was made Poet Laureate, but his uniqueness as a writer had been apparent from a very early stage in his career. 'He has,' said Maurice Bowra in the early 1930s, 'a mind of extraordinary originality; there is no one else remotely like him.' This distinctiveness makes the world of Betjeman's poems and prose sketches an immediately recognizable one: a world of seaside piers and country golf-clubs, cottage hospitals and Spa Pavilions, tennis courts and tea-shops, sleepy railway branch lines with gas-lit station platforms. The style of his verse is unpretentious (most of his poems had their first draft on the back of a cigarette packet or in the margins of old letters), with an easy simplicity concealing a sharp sense of irony, or a penetrating criticism of the hollowness and philistinism of modern life.

His poem 'Christmas', from the 1954 collection **A Few Late Chrysanthemums***, contains the kind of homely detail so characteristic of his work, such as the Tortoise stove (this was a cast-iron stove for heating large buildings like churches, and it carried the trade-mark of a tortoise with the slogan 'slow but sure'). At the same time his message is direct and uncompromising: the affirmation of the central tenet of Christianity in a world which tends to ignore it.*

The bells of waiting Advent ring,
    The Tortoise stove is lit again
And lamp-oil light across the night
    Has caught the streaks of winter rain
In many a stained-glass window sheen
From Crimson Lake to Hooker's Green.

The holly in the windy hedge
    And round the Manor house the yew
Will soon be stripped to deck the ledge,
    The altar, font and arch and pew,
So that the villagers can say
'The church looks nice' on Christmas Day.

Provincial public houses blaze
   And Corporation tramcars clang,
On lighted tenements I gaze
   Where paper decorations hang,
And bunting in the red Town Hall
Says 'Merry Christmas to you all.'

And London shops on Christmas Eve
   Are strung with silver bells and flowers
As hurrying clerks the City leave
   To pigeon-haunted classic towers,
And marbled clouds go scudding by
The many-steepled London sky.

And girls in slacks remember Dad,
   And oafish louts remember Mum,
And sleepless children's hearts are glad,
   And Christmas-morning bells say 'Come!'
Even to shining ones who dwell
Safe in the Dorchester Hotel.

And is it true? And is it true,
   This most tremendous tale of all,
Seen in a stained-glass window's hue,
   A Baby in an ox's stall?
The Maker of the stars and sea
Become a Child on earth for me?

And is it true? For if it is,
   No loving fingers tying strings
Around those tissued fripperies,
   The sweet and silly Christmas things,
Bath salts and inexpensive scent
And hideous tie so kindly meant,

No love that in a family dwells,
   No carolling in frosty air,
Nor all the steeple-shaking bells
   Can with this single Truth compare –
That God was Man in Palestine
And lives today in Bread and Wine.